MW00720384

THE DEVIL

DRIVES

A ROMANTIC HISTORICAL ADVENTURE

BY

EDWARD PAYNE

Hookway
Publishing Co.

When The Devil Drives
Copyright © 2010 by Edward Payne

All rights reserved. No part of this publication may be reproduced, stored in a retrieval system, rebound or transmitted in any form or by any means, electronic, mechanical, photocopying, recording or otherwise, without prior written permission of the author and publisher. This book is sold subject to condition that it shall not by way of trade or otherwise be resold, hired out or otherwise circulated without the publisher's prior consent in any form of binding or cover other than that in which it was published.

The events and characters depicted in this book are fictitious. Any similarity to actual persons, living or dead, is purely coincidental.

Edited by John Lederman
Design and layout by John Lederman

Typeface: Didot and Garamond

Published by
Hookway Publishing Company
1118 N. Blair Ave., Royal Oak, MI, 48067

Printed in the USA by
Page Litho, Inc.
6445 East Vernor, Detroit, MI, 48207

ISBN 978-0-9842941-0-7

This book is dedicated to my father, who returned from the war, and like so many others, sometimes wished he hadn't.

Hit ys oft seyde by hem that yet lyues He must nedys go that
the deuell dryues.

> *c* 1450, J. Lydgate *Assembly of Gods* (EETS) l. 21

He must needs go that the devil drives.

> 1602, Shakespeare *All's Well that ends Well* I. iii. 29

Contents

PREFACE

IN THOSE DAYS, BRITISH AMBULANCES WERE HIGH, SQUARE, AND WHITE, WITH A LARGE CROSS OF ST. GEORGE ON THE SIDES. THEY CARRIED A BELL MOUNTED ON THE FRONT BUMPER THAT MADE A HIGH-PITCHED TRILLING RING AS THE VEHICLE SPED ALONG THE STREETS AND HIGHWAYS. THIS ONE, BEARING ITS PATIENT, AND GOING A LITTLE FASTER THAN SAFETY ALLOWED, MADE ITS WAY FROM THE LITTLE AIRFIELD AT LYMPNE, THROUGH THE GREEN FOLDS OF KENT, ON ITS WAY TO LONDON.

INSIDE, THE FIGURE ON THE STRETCHER OPENED HIS EYES, MOVED A HAND, AND TRIED TO SPEAK. HIS BLISTERED, CRACKED, AND SWOLLEN LIPS MOVED. A CROAK CAME OUT. ONE OF THE ATTENDANTS SAID,
" 'EES WAKING UP GEORGE."
THE OTHER MAN, THE SENIOR, SPOKE,
"IT'S ALRIGHT SIR. YOU'RE SAFE IN ENGLAND NOW."

CECIL DRIFTED BACK INTO BLESSED OBLIVION, DREAMING. HE WAS BACK HOME BEING ADMONISHED: TO BE A BETTER SCHOLAR, TO APPLY HIMSELF MORE ASSIDUOUSLY TO HIS LESSONS. IT WAS THE SAME OLD STORY, HIS FATHER'S VAGUELY ANXIOUS FACE, HIS OWN FEELINGS OF INADEQUACY, OF LACK OF INITIATIVE, OF LIVING IN A DREAM WORLD...

EARLY LIFE...

It seemed as though Cecil's Paynter's life up to now was principally spent trying to please his father, who hardly knew who he was half the time, and would peer at him absently as though he was a stranger most of the time. His father was generally quite kind, but spent more time and concern on his stamp collection and his butterfly and insect collection. The only other intercourse was when they had a monthly meeting in his father's study. This was a formal arrangement and would take a definite planned course.

The program would begin with a strictly timed interview, questions pertaining to progress at school, health, and general welfare, then a lecture on morals and religious practice, an updated version of what books should be read and what books should not, then emolument would be distributed, his monthly allowance, known to Cecil and his sister as the widow's mite. He would then be dismissed and attention would be turned back to stamps and bugs.

His mother was even worse. When he was going to his prep school, which was in Nottingham and which he attended as a boarder, she would, very rarely, visit him, and when she did, would cause an uproar by turning up be-jewelled and be-furred and smelling of very expensive perfume. She was still quite youthful-looking and, in fact, something of a beauty. She would arrive, extravagantly, by chauffeured limousine. She would charm all the masters and the little boys, perfunctorily kiss Cecil, then sweep away to tea with the headmaster and be gone by dark.

Cecil's only real comfort at home was his sister, stunning, like her mother, but with a heart that she shared with Cecil. She would write to him and send him news and small amounts of money, which would be spent on books and sweets. He adored her. When he was on holiday he spent most of his time with her. She would take him to all the museums and galleries in Edinburgh, which was a short railway trip from where they lived in the lake district county of Cumberland, where they lived in a Georgian house that nestled in the dark hills of north western England.

Cecil had a brother, Nigel, who was five years his junior and who spent all his time playing cricket in the summer and rugby in the winter and wasn't a bit interested with books or any other form of intellectual activity. They had nothing whatsoever in common. And it didn't help Cecil's lack of self confidence to be aware that Nigel was the family favourite.

They lived in the comparative comfort of the late Edwardian period, a time that was to turn out as the calm before the storm. The house was big enough, and they had enough money to warrant and afford servants. There was a housekeeper, a cook, and two maids. Outside there was a gardener. Cecil would spend his days, when there, reading in the panelled library where there was always a fire going. For exercise, which he didn't particularly enjoy, but which was forced upon him, he would walk the flowered woods and hills that surrounded the house. Days and months passed in a sort of gentle sylvan dream.

The summer that year was especially warm, sunny, and un-English. None of them were particularly aware of what was going on in the rest of the world. They were vaguely pleased that most of it was pink on the maps and that their little country owned or ran most of it, kindly and honourably. They were certain that all those funny little foreign people just loved producing much of the food they ate and no doubt lived in plain and simple, but adequate, households. Yes, life was pretty good all round.

The year was 1913 and Cecil would be leaving his prep school and going to his public school, which, because they belonged to the old faith, was Catholic. It was run and staffed by Benedictine monks, the headquarters of whose order was at Monte Cassino in Italy.

Then an obscure duke was assassinated in August 1914 in an even more obscure town in a completely unknown part of the world and all the fears, suspicions, and hatreds of old Europe tumbled down the fragile, complex, and generally unworkable structure of treaties, arrangements, and family relationships. These were torn up and consigned to files that would never be opened again. The royal cousins would address each other politely in the arcane language of the diplomacy of the time, then never speak again to each other. And then, most of Europe fell head over heels into war.

Cecil went to his school, and though of a timid and sensitive disposition, wished he was going to war instead. After all, this was a just struggle in his opinion, and would, all the teachers said, be over by Christmas. His feeling of dislike and suspicion of Germany and the Kaiser only reflected the feelings of most of the citizens of Great Britain.

This optimism was ill-founded. Nineteen fifteen came and went, and late in nineteen sixteen he was old enough to volunteer and be accepted for training as an infantry officer at Sandhurst. Not much time would elapse before he found himself, at the front.

FOREIGN FIELDS...

Cecil peered over the parapet. The rain drumming on his helmet dribbled over the brim onto his nose. He wiped his cuff across his face, cursing the day, the place, and his bad luck in being there. His company sergeant major growled "Shall I get the men ready sah?"

"No sergeant. Hang on a bit. I can't quite see if the wire's cut." At that moment a bullet zinged through the air and plopped into the parados behind his head. He ducked.

"Steady sir." The NCO tugged at his arm.

"Alright sarge. No harm done." He looked around and behind him. The men of his company were huddled in the trench, a muddied khaki group, their rifles sticking up in a haphazard untidy way, anxious pink faces peering about.

It was dawn, it was winter, it was cold. It was northern France. The year was 1916. The fashion of the day was to aggressively patrol. This was the dictum handed down from staff headquarters. Woe betide any battalion that kept their heads down and tried to lie quietly as some of the French did. The colonel would be quickly summoned onto the carpet and advised to change his ways, or be replaced. Disgrace or worse would be his lot. Thus it was that Cecil's regiment, a lowland Scottish new army battalion, was carrying out these orders, and he was, so to speak, at the sharp end of the stick.

He slumped down and fumbled for a cigarette. The sergeant lit it with a kitchen match.

"Thanks Johnson. Well, let the men relax for a bit until things calm down and this bloody rain stops."

"Right sir. Awlright, stand easy." The sergeant's bellow brought smiles of relief to the men's faces. Fag ends glowed. Overhead, machine gun rounds went through the wire ricochetting. Tapocket, tapocket, tapocket. A five point nine shell burst in No-Man's Land hurling mud and debris in all directions. He took a deep drag at the cigarette and tried to stop his shaking hand from being too obvious to the sergeant who was looking at him with anxiety.

'Christ,' he thought. 'It just seems like the other day I was going out to bat in the game against Douai. I was shaking a bit then, but all they were throwing at me then were cricket balls. God, that was a fast one that got me and sent me walking disconsolately back to the pavilion to hear the usual "hard luck old boy." "Hard cheese old chap." Averted eyes. The "Jolly good shows." Damn! cricket could be so humiliating... . Oh well.'

"Any cucumber sandwiches left?"

"Sir. Sir." The sergeant was shaking his arm. Cecil was miles away at the cricket match.

"What, what? I was just resting my eyes."

"It's the adjutant sir. He's just around the comer."

"Right. 'Tenshun."

The adjutant, a short, stocky, red-faced, bad-tempered

officer, came into sight accompanied by his assistant.

"Why the hell aren't you over there?" He nodded towards the parapet.

"Sorry sir. Just going over. Yes, just getting ready to go. Right. Sar'nt, over we go." Cecil tugged at his revolver holster, and trying to look martial, began to scramble up the ladder.

What light there was, cast a baleful glare over the scene of desolation. Churned up ground littered with splintered wood, rusty wire, bits of corrugated iron, all the detritus of war, lay about. Shell holes full almost to the brim with what looked like cold pea-green soup, but which smelled of death.

He gazed about him carefully. With much more noise and fuss than was really necessary, the rest of the patrol clustered behind him. These were new drafts who had only been out a week. They kept together, as tyros in battle do. They would learn, if they survived, to keep apart in future.

"Sar'nt. Take three men and go that way. I'll take Corporal Jones and Private, er... Mathews, isn't it? and work around to the left. Meet you in..." he checked the time... "in fifteen minutes at the ruined farm. Let's see what we can see." He crawled away down the slope that led toward the German front line.

The early morning hate had ended and in the comparative quiet, the men on both sides were preparing their breakfasts – one of the reasons this particular time had been chosen for their expedition.

A silly bird chirruped in the distance. The odd crump from some shell exploded far away. A mound of shattered bricks, the remains of a house, gave him a little shelter, so that he could sit up and very carefully look through his binoculars at the enemy line. Smoke was rising from the cooking fires, something that was fairly rare in this sector of the line. But apparently the length of trench had been taken over by Saxons who were disposed to live and let live.

He sat back and contemplated the situation. The object of these patrols was the gaining of information. If lucky, the capture of a soldier. If very lucky, the capture of an officer. Other scenarios could include the exchange of fire at close range, perhaps a Mill's bomb chucked down a dugout step, anything to annoy Jerry and keep him on edge.

"Well bugger that. I think a return with some information about the sparseness of the Germans' presence in the front line will suffice today. After all, I am on leave to England next week. Let's get back."

As if to encourage this move, a couple of rounds placked into the wall, sending up rosy dust from their impact.

"Fuck. I'm gone. Come on lads. Let's go home." They scrabbled up the way they had come, a now thoroughly roused German trench blazing away.

Reaching the battered buildings of the ruined farm by more circuitous routes, they arrived late, to find a rather alarmed sergeant.

"Cor. We thought you'd 'ad it sir. We 'eard the shooting."

"No, no. All's well. Anything to report from your end?"

"No sir. We 'ad a cushy time."

8

"Good. Let's get back. I'm ready for breakfast.

After they had all flopped back into the comparative safety of their trench, and he had dismissed the men to their food, Cecil hurried to the dugout housing the company HQ. Hurried was hardly the word to use. His progress was hampered by booted feet sticking out of excavated holes in the sides of the trench: men off duty, sleeping, their bodies covered by tarpaulin sheets. Working parties dug at the squishing mud that threatened to overwhelm them all. Sandbags, repaired, were being slung over the top to those waiting to stack. Duckboards underfoot, broken and imperfect, waited to catch the unwary foot.

Finally the curtained entry to HQ was reached. He pulled the canvas to one side and went down a short flight of earthen steps. There was another heavy gas-proof sheet at the bottom. He pulled it to one side to be greeted with a chorus of, "Keep the fucking door shut."

"Sodding hell. Don't bring all that bloody cold in here."

"What's up Paynter? Thought you were on leave. Had breakfast yet?"

"No. Give us a cup of tea? Christ, it's cold out there. He shivered.

"Ah, Paynter." An older man with the three pips of a captain on his shoulders looked up from some papers he was studying. "Doing your bit to keep his nibs happy this morning?"

"Yes sir. Went out for a morning stroll. Bit of a waste of time I'm afraid. Didn't see much. There's hardly anyone over there?"

"Oh really? Well all the other platoons have been over and come back. They all report the same thing."

'That's a relief,' thought Cecil.

"Okay, have your tea and get some sleep. Something big is coming up. You're going home soon, aren't you?"

"Yes sir. Next Monday."

"Right. Go and enjoy yourself. You should be back in time for the fun."

'Damn. I was hoping I'd miss it,' Cecil said to himself.

"Oh, that's capital Sir. Wouldn't want to miss that."

He stumbled back up the stairs. It was now full daylight. Some friendly artillery rounds went whining overhead. There was a battery of eighteen pounders not far behind them, and every time they fired a few shots at Gerry, he answered with twice as many, all falling amongst the infantry.

'Wish they wouldn't do that,' he thought. Ah, here we are. Home at last.' He practically fell down the steps into his little hole in the ground.

Actually it was quite cosy. His batman, who was there to greet him with some tepid tea liberally spiced with whisky, had found some planks and walled up the bare earth sides. These were covered with pictures from some French magazines featuring very pretty girls in black knickers and very little else. There was an open brazier in one corner sending clouds of woody, acrid smoke in all directions. A rough, wooden table with a couple of battered chairs completed the furnishings. A frying pan, crackling with bacon, and bread, sat insecurely on the embers. Cecil struggled out of his equipment. Sam Browne, holster, field glasses, gas mask, overcoat, boots, jacket.

Billings, his servant, handed him an old woolen jumper that he pulled on. He sat and lit a cigarette. Sipping the tea, he looked around. His chums, two other officers he shared with, were gone on other duties, so he had the place to himself. He ate the greasy, but satisfying meal, had another cigarette, and rolled himself up in a blanket. Turning to the wall, he closed his eyes and fell into a deep untroubled sleep.

LOOKING FORWARD, HARKING BACK...

The next few days dragged interminably. His chums tried to make things easier for him, doing the odd duty in his place, and allowing him to sleep longer than he should. His batman was, as always, a tower of strength, as was his sergeant, who, as in most armies, really ran things. He was an old soldier, sporting ribbons on his number one tunic, showing that he had served in India, the Sudan, and South Africa.

Cecil thought about the circumstances that had brought him to this point in his life. Last year he had done his time at Sandhurst, the Army school that churned out young officers so badly needed for the growing army of amateur soldiers. Casualties amongst infantry officers, being what they were, life expectancy was short, but if one survived, promotion was speedy.

The year before that, Cecil was studying at his public school, a Benedictine upper class establishment that sat on a hill above the city of Bath, educating boys for the Church, the Government, Colonial Services, and the Law – until, that is, 1914, when the graduates were all sent to the slaughter of the war, including the sons of foreign princes being educated in England who finished up on the side of the enemy, their comfy English sojourn with cucumber sandwiches, Pimms Cup, and debutantes interrupted brutally by the conflict.

After passing at Sandhurst with average marks, and asked which regiment he preferred (within reason, his marks not allowing him to try for the Guards or the Rifle Regiments) he chose first, any light infantry or fusilier regiments. Happily they sent him to the 6th Battalion of the Royal Scots Fusiliers, the 21st of Foot, quite respectable in the regimental pecking order. Winston Churchill had commanded a battalion the previous year.

The regiment was in the line near Festubert and one rainy, gloomy day Cecil was being trundled along in a very uncomfortable troop train packed to the roofs with cursing sweating soldiers, until they reached the railhead and were deposited on a crumbling platform to find their respective units and guides, which somehow was done, and Cecil found himself trudging along with the rest of the draft on a muddy broken road lined with shattered trees and the remnants of houses.

It was getting dark when the guide stopped and motioned the group down some steps that led into a shallow communication trench.

"Ere we are sir. Regent Street. This takes you straight to your headquarters. Good luck sir."

"Thanks for your help and good luck to you," Cecil replied.

At a sudden clatter of horses and equipment they were splashed with mud and a shower of stones as an artillery battery went past them going hell for leather down the road. Cecil ducked.

"That's right Sir. Learn how to get your 'ed down when you 'ave to." The soldier chuckled. "I'd put my 'elmet on too sir, if I was you. We're in range 'ere." He turned away and disappeared into the darkness.

Cecil turned to the remainder of the draft he was with and said, "Right. Helmets on. Chin straps down. All ready? Off we go then. Follow me."

He pulled his collar up and started down the dark corridor of muddy earth, the darkness only fitfully lit at irregular intervals by star shells arcing up into the cloudy gloom with shattering bursts of brilliance.

By the time he found the battalion HQ, it was quite dark, but after a couple of false turns and being sworn at by sleeping men he trod on, he did find it, and was welcomed with much cheerfulness by the occupants, two young subalterns like himself, and a wire-haired terrier which jumped into his lap and licked his face while Cecil tried to drink a whiskey that his new friends had thrust into his hand.

"I'm Patterson and this wart is Murray, one of the few Scotsmen in this company." They shook hands. "The dog's Archy. He likes you. That's good."

"Billings," the older of the two officers yelled in the general direction of a blanket that hung on one wall.

"Sir!"

The blanket was pulled back from the other side revealing a stocky, red-faced, older soldier framed in a rough doorway that led into another space from which came the scents of cooking and paraffin oil.

"Billings, this is our new officer. Second Lieutenant Paynter, this is the incomparable Billings, who looks after us."

"How d'you do Billings?"

"Ow d'yer do Sir? I 'ope you'll be comfy with us Sir. Will you be 'aving supper?"

"Absolutely. Smells wonderful."

Dinner was wonderful. Billings was, apparently, one of the regiment's best scroungers. Cecil was to live quite well in the days to come, at least in the food department.

Sleep came quickly that night... .

Next day, Cecil was introduced to the other officers and to the platoon of men he was to command and be responsible for. Most of them were roughly his age, but some were older. His sergeant was an old regular and was to be his right arm and his strength in the trials to come.

After a day or two Cecil was requested, quite politely, he thought, to attend on his Commanding Officer. He trembled at the thought. The great man had an awesome reputation.

At the appointed hour, a gruff voice said, "Come in," when he knocked on the wooden frame of the dugout door. He entered the earthen cavern.

"Paynter, Sir. Reporting, Sir," he stuttered.

The officer had the new shoulder rank badges. They used to be largely on the cuffs, until too many of them were killed by snipers. The badges indicated the rank of Lieutenant Colonel.

He looked up from some papers he was reading and said,

"Stand at ease Paynter. Sit down. Sit down." He indicated a battered chair. Cecil sat.

"Tell me about yourself."

Cecil, taken aback by this unexpected amiability, sat after a moment. He tried to be brief, sensing this was the preferred tactic. Least said, etc., etc. ... .

"Ah yes," said the illustrious one. "Well, this is a good battalion. We're a little tired. Been out since Loos and Neuve Chapelle, so that's not surprising. Have you met the other officers and your men?"

"Yes Sir, I have."

"Good. Now you know your first duty here is to your men. Make sure they are in good health and spirits. Lead by example."

There was a pause.

"Pay especial attention to their feet."

After this surprising statement, he added, "These ex-coal miners are very lazy about changing into dry socks. Make sure that they do."

"Right."

"We're in a quiet sector here, so you can learn the ropes in comparative peace and quiet."

At that moment there was a shrieking, moaning sound ending in an enormous crash causing the front door to shudder and blowing earth and stones down the steps. Cecil crouched in fear and trembling.

"It's alright Paynter. No harm done."

Cecil looked up from his position of undignified alarm

and saw the great one tamping some tobacco into his pipe with a look of calm detachment.

"You may go now. Come and see me in a week or so and we'll talk some more. Good luck my boy." He turned back to his papers looking for all the world like Cecil's history master at school, even to the clouds of aromatic smoke that now surrounded his grizzled head. Cecil saluted and ran up the steps two at a time.

BEGINNING LEAVE...

Finally the great day for his leave to England arrived. Cecil made his way, accompanied by Billings, who was also going on leave, up the communication trench that meandered back to the rear. The day was clear and skylarks sang in the blue above. There was an occasional shell burst in the distance. Otherwise it was a quiet day.

They reached the village in the middle of the day, or what there was left of it. A small group of Highlanders were hanging about in a group, smoking. They came to attention.

"Carry on," said Cecil. They relaxed and continued smoking and chatting. A lorry drove up.

"Leave party for Albert?" The driver hung out of the old vehicle.

"Right. All aboard for Blighty."

A long, bumpy, chilly two hours passed, then onto the troop train for the channel coast, then the short but uncomfortable, seasick-making crossing to Dover. It was too dark to see the cliffs, although they glowed whitely above the docks as they debarked.

They reached London's Charing Cross station, at midnight. The train stopped, the doors creaking and crashing. Sleepy, tired, but happy troops debouched onto the platform.

Cecil joined the multitude and headed for the concourse. He passed the snorting, steaming, grimy-green locomotive. The two black faces of the driver and fireman split with white-toothed grins.

"Good luck mates," they shouted.

Outside, the inevitable rain was streaming down. Cecil got into an ancient Beardmore taxi.

"The Ritz Hotel please."

"Right sir." The heavily moustached driver touched his cap, started up, and drove out into the traffic, coursing down the Strand. Cecil leaned back with a sigh of relief and lit a cigarette. He couldn't really afford it, but he had determined to spend at least one night at one of the better London hotels.

When they arrived, the taxi door was flung open with a flourish by a uniformed commissionaire.

"Good evening sir."

Cecil paid off the driver. He included a rather overly generous tip.

"Thank you kindly sir. 'Ave a good leave."

After a long and luxurious hot bath, Cecil dressed in his number ones. His regimentals were typical of the Lowland Scottish units, consisting of a khaki tunic and tartan trews, the pattern of which was known as the government tartan: dark green with dark blue and black checks. He looked exceedingly handsome. Dashing even.

As he passed the hall mirror, he couldn't help glancing at his reflection. He grinned. 'Not bad. Look out London.'

Entering the dining room, he looked about. The

beautiful chandeliered room, sparkling with light and diamonds, was packed with diners and dancers. Waiters dashed around balancing piled-up trays. Music played gaily. Women were dressed in glittering long dresses. Tiaras were on every head. Jewellery gleamed and shone everywhere. Most men were in uniform, some in mess kit, some in evening dress.

"Good evening sir, a table for one?"

"Yes, I'm afraid so."

"Of course. This way sir, this way." The captain led the way threading through the tables.

It seemed all London was celebrating here tonight. Cecil thought of where he had been yesterday and shivered. This all seemed so surreal.

"Jesus Christ. Paynter! What the hell are you doing here?"

He looked around. It was an old school chum, John Heatherington!

"How are you Heathers?"

"Spot of leave you know. Are you alone Cecil?"

"Yes, dammit. Just got in."

"Well we can't have that, can we girls?" He looked at two very pretty young women sitting at the table.

"All right. Maitre de. We'll look after him. Meet Fiona, my sister up from Cheltenham for the Easter hols, and this is my special girl Nichola."

"Er, how d'you do?" Cecil said.

"Hello." They both looked up, smiling and enchanting.

"I say, waiter. Bring another bottle of Bolly." Heathers

motioned to a hovering waiter, who, with the alacrity of a conjurer, produced the black crested bottle, silently ejected the cork, and began to pour.

The remainder of the night was a blur of laughing mouths, soft pliant bodies, music, and dancing. There was a short but hectic drive in an open car of some impressive power and discomfort, a clumsy and unsuccessful attempt at some sort of sexual connection, then the magic ended with an assisted entry to the hotel.

Feeling not a little fragile, Cecil woke from a heavy and troubled sleep the next morning. Opening one bleary eye he tried to focus on the alarm clock that he had forgotten to set the night before.

"Damn, blast, and buggery." He was going to miss his train. "Christ!"

He reeled from a piercing headache and almost passed out. Grabbing the back of a chair for support, he took a deep breath and looked about. His clothes were in a pile on the chair, his bag lying on the floor spilling its contents.

"OK. Take a grip. Where's the bathroom? Ah, here we are."

'Basin taps on. No time for bath. Quick shave. Wet cloth under the armpits and around the privates,' (what was called, in typical English jargon of the day, a Frenchman's wash). 'Bit of brilliantine for the hair.' Feeling better. 'Whoa! Forgot the teeth.' The flat round tin of dentifrice, a solid cake of pumice-like substance, barely invented, which one applied to the brush and then scrubbed on the teeth, and which tasted of mint, was found, and the process of recovery proceeded.

Dressed, packed, and feeling better, he got on the creaky elaborate cage-like lift and descended to the ground floor. Luckily, the hour still being early, the process of booking out was fast, and in no time he was in a taxi heading to Euston Station.

The great glass and iron structure loomed ahead, looking, in the London fog, like some monstrous antediluvian mammoth. The entrance, ill lit and in darkness, gaped unwelcomingly to the traveler en route to Scotland and the north.

"Flying Scot sir?" the driver, capped, with a drooping, tobacco-stained walrus moustache and scarlet nose, enquired.

"Yes please."

"Right sir." The old cab that smelled of horse piss and straw growled to a stop alongside a platform swarming with troops and sailors.

Smoke and steam filled the air, hissing and swirling, almost obscuring a long line of carriages, grimy and travel-stained, at the far end of which, was a massive steam locomotive in livery of dark red, black, and gold, clanking and boiling.

This was the London Midland and Scottish Railway Company's Flying Scot, the crack express of the day, and which would be Cecil's home for the next several hours.

" 'Ere we are sir." The porter, who had appeared from nowhere and grabbed his bags, opened a door in the first class section. "Nice and cosy. Smoking I think?

"Yes."

Bags up 'ere," he said, swinging the luggage onto racks.

Accepting the emolument Cecil pressed into his hand the porter said, "Thank you sir. Good luck sir." The door slammed shut.

'God, that's better.' Cecil relaxed against the seat back and lit a cigarette. 'Piece of luck. An empty compartment.'

Just as he thought that, the door to the corridor slid open with a crash and a red-faced perspiring porter said, " 'Scuse me sir," and deposited a large portmanteau on the rack above his head and backed out allowing a pretty young woman to enter.

She said. " D'you mind?" and with a rustle of taffeta skirts, sat down opposite. She regarded him cooly and quickly and looked out of the window.

The whistle started to blow as the guards began the process of alerting the driver and fireman and passengers to the imminence of departure. Doors slammed along the train. The engine hooted its signal to the world, and with a lurch, moved forward. The platform and its contents, the impedimenta of stations everywhere, were passed: milk churns, hampers, barrows with mountains of boxes. Figures in black with pink faces glided by, faster and faster, and eventually blurring into the mists and fogs of the world outside the station. As the train emerged, it clacked across the complex of points, swaying and jerking from side to side, and then quickly plunged into the black stygian darkness of a tunnel.

At that moment the door to the corridor slid open again and a tall burly figure entered.

"Hello darling," said the girl.

"Hello my dear," a deep gruff voice answered.

"Almost got our own compartment," the girl said with some petulance.

"Yes," the man's voice replied.

"Bloody nuisance, what?"

"Well I'm frightfully sorry," said Cecil, "but I was here first. We shall just have to make the best of it."

"What are you, army or navy?" the gruff voice asked. It was still dark, and faces and figures were indistinct.

"Army. Worst luck. I wish I had gone into the bloody navy. Sitting about in the mud in France is not my cup of tea. Being bossed about by a bunch of old idiots on the staff who don't know what they are doing is really too bad." The train swept with a roar out of the tunnel and into the grey but bright light outside. Then Cecil saw the insignia. 'God in Heaven! It's a general!'

"Oh dear sir. I'm terribly sorry. I had no idea." A major general according to his shoulder epaulettes, pips, and crowns, with bushy moustache and eyebrows to suit, sat, frowning, red-faced, and fierce, facing him. The girl was grinning from ear to attractive ear.

"So you're a Scots Fusilier.

"Yes sir," said Cecil, briskly sitting to attention.

"Ninth battalion."

"Yes sir."

"Yes. You're in my division."

'Oh God this is getting worse.'

"Billingsley your OC?"

"Yes sir."

"Well you're lucky I'm on leave and with my daughter. Otherwise you would be mending docks in Brittany tomorrow. Alright. As you were," he smiled transforming himself into a rather genial looking, old gentleman. "Like a cigarette?"

Cecil accepted with profuse thanks.

"Where are you going my boy?"

"To stay with my family in Penrith, sir.

"Ah."

"And you sir?" Cecil embraced the daughter with this question. She smiled.

"We are going to my house in Scotland," replied the general. At that moment the door opened and a steward looked in. "Lunch is served in ten minutes sir."

"Right. We'll be right along."

Later, seated at a table in the dining car, Cecil, who had gone on ahead, contemplated the menu. As usual, food on the long distant trains was first class. He decided on the Dover sole with new potatoes and runner beans, with strawberries and cream for pudding.

"Ah." He drew deeply on his cigarette and inhaled luxuriously. The train swayed gently. The clickety-clack sound reminded him vaguely of machine gun fire. He sipped from the glass of sauterne. 'God. if the lads could see me now.'

"May we join you?" It was the general and daughter.

"Of course sir. Delighted." He sprang to his feet with alacrity, almost knocking over the wine bucket.

"Something to drink sir?" It was the steward.

"Yes. Darling what would you like?

"Er, I think a gin and French."

"Capital. I think I'll have the same."

"The menu sir." A deferential passing of gold embossed card.

"Thank you. "What are you having Paynter?"

"Sole sir."

"Looks good. I'll have the same. Rowena?"

"No, I just want an omelet."

"Right, right."

Cecil looked out of the window at the countryside passing by. It was pelting rain and the glass was streaked, making the view indistinct.

"Bit gloomy, what? What time do we get to your stop? Shouldn't be long now, should it?"

"We'll be there in about three hours sir."

"Yes, that sounds right."

"We get to Carlisle at midnight then change to a puffer that takes us to Stranraer."

The drinks arrived. Glasses were raised and clinked.

"When do you go back to France?"

"Next week, sir."

"Yes, well, if you have time, come and visit us for a day or two. We have good shooting and fishing."

Deciding not to mention his distinct aversion to either pastime, but keeping his mind on the main chance, Cecil said, "Delighted sir. Thank you." He caught the girl's eye. She smiled.

The grim spine of England was darkening as the train strained up Shap Fell, part of the Pennine Chain, the ridge that divides the damp Atlantic winds from the dry cold airs of Russia.

The summit reached, the driver began to apply brakes and turn the valves that lessened the pressures driving the wheels. The fireman began the processes of dampening down the glowing coals as the train started its descent to Penrith.

"Goodbye my boy. Have a good leave. Perhaps we shall see you next week."

"Thank you sir." He turned to Rowena. "Goodbye."

"No, I won't say goodbye, *au revoir* perhaps. Do try to come to Scotland. It's not far." She looked appealingly into his eyes and softly squeezed his hand.

"I'll try, really."

SCOTLAND AND THE FAMILY...

It was still raining gently as Cecil stepped onto the platform. A light mist lay about. A porter approached.

"Your bags sir?"

"Yes please. I think I'm being met."

"Yes sir. This way to the parking lot, this way."

A tall figure detached itself from the throngs of people milling about. "Is it Cecil?"

"Yes. Hello Nigel." It was his younger brother, not old enough for the services yet. Hopefully he might just miss the carnage.

"How was the journey?"

"Rather jolly actually." He gave an abbreviated version of his adventures.

"Jammy bugger. Those sort of things never happen to me."

"How's mother?"

"Not bad. A bit worried about servants and food supplies and so on. The usual thing. You know how she is."

"And Father?"

"Oh busy as can be. Municipal stuff. His stamp collection, and of course, his bugs, and not knowing where he is half the time, old duffer. ("His bugs" were a collection of domestic and exotic butterflies which was actually world renowned.)

"And Molly?"

"Oh she's fine. Working with the local hospital and having a great time with bandages, splints, and boracic powder, plus breaking every military heart that goes through the place."

"Good for her."

"Here's the car." An enormous black Lanchester stood, attended by a uniformed chauffeur.

"Good evening Master Paynter."

"Good evening Johnson. How are you?"

"Very well sir. Allow me sir." He spread a blanket across Cecil's knees.

The door shut with a satisfying thunk. Nigel twisted around from the front seat. "Is it hell over there?"

"Yes," replied Cecil and lit a cigarette. The car glided through the shining wet streets of the town, deserted now at this late hour. The buildings and houses thinned out as they went through the outskirts and then there was just open moorland. The headlights arced through the dark mist ahead.

Cecil gazed at the passing, black, looming hills and thought, 'Christ I'm tired.' A few more miles of broken moors and then some trees. The road wound through these and came to a white gate which it passed through and swept up a winding, gravelled drive. A large Georgian house came into view. It was in darkness except for a dim light in one of the front rooms.

The car came to a crunching stop at the front of the house and the main door opened, flooding the outside with light. Silhouetted against this was a figure, slightly stooped, with a walking stick.

"Father! How super to see you."

"Ah, my boy. Splendid, splendid. Yes, well.., well.., come in, come in." They walked into the warm hallway. The usual clutter of coats, hats, sticks, and boots was negotiated.

"Would you like a drink? I think we have some sherry somewhere. Or perhaps a sandwich? Yes? You must be famished."

This unexpected hospitality took Cecil by surprise. Father seemed to have gone through a seminal change. He appeared to know who Cecil was, and, was being kind and welcoming. 'Oh well. whatever it is I like it' thought Cecil.

"It's alright father. I'm fine. Just want bed. Same room?"

"Yes. I believe Mrs, er, what's her name? has prepared it. Well, off you go. See you in the morning."

"Good night father, Nigel."

He climbed the stairs, wearily holding the banister for support. At the top of the stairs the hall extended in both directions. He turned right, down the old familiar corridor lined with fox hunting prints, to his old nursery door. Here he paused. There was only one light in the hallway, a wall sconce that gave a dim glow to the passage. In just the few seconds he was still, thoughts and memories came rushing back: his nanny, Mrs Thompson, who was universally adored, echoed "Now now, master Cecil." The kindly scolding voice; laughter from a thousand moments of childhood pranks and japes; Guy Fawkes night; the fog and sparklers; Catherine wheels and Roman candles; the first Hornby Railway set; the games of sardines and murder; ...faces ... voices. 'God, this is too much. Pull things together,' Cecil thought. 'Don't go there.'

He opened the door and turned on the light. The room had been made into a bedroom, comfortably furnished, but as in most houses in England, icy. He unbuttoned his tunic and flung it on a chair. Undoing his collar and tie, he walked to the bed. 'Oh great.' A stone hot water bottle lay there snugly toasting the sheets. He removed all clothing and put on his pyjamas. 'Quick brush of the teeth and into the bed.' Cold, except for the little nub of warmth in the middle. He turned on one side, stretched legs, mumbled a couple of Hail Marys, and slipped into blessed unconsciousness.

The sound of a clinking cup and saucer for the morning tea being placed by his bed, woke him. The swoosh and clatter of curtains being drawn and the bright light of the sun streaming into the room made him open his eyes and blink,, he saw a pretty, rosy cheeked maid in blue and white, she bobbed in a quick curtsey.

"Morning young master. Breakfast ready soon."

"Oh, yes, thank you. Er, up in a thrice. Morning, morning."

She swept out of the room with a rustling sound, leaving behind the scent of fresh air, lavender soap, and coffee.

Having completed his toilet, Cecil descended the stairs and entered the dining room. His mother and father, at either end of long table, looked up and smiled.

"Morning my boy," said father.

"Kiss, kiss," said mother.

Father retired behind boiled eggs and the Telegraph, snorting.

"Did you sleep well?" Asked ma-ma.

"Like a dead horse."

She made a *moué* of distaste. "Oh dear, you've become rather coarse since you joined the army. I do hope this won't be a permanent habit."

"Frightfully sorry mother."

"Oh, it's alright. Everything is changing now. You should see what I have to put up with, what with rationing and all. And no help. My dear the young people are quite impossible to deal with today. It's just so difficult to keep the house nice and have parties and so on. All the men over in France cavorting about having a good time. I really do not know how we are supposed to manage." She absent mindedly spooned mouthfuls of porridge into her mouth and gazed out of the window.

"I am sorry things are so difficult for you ma-ma. Perhaps things will get better soon. Where's Nigel?"

"Oh, he's staying with his chum Julian Thompson. You remember the Thompsons. A bit nouveau, live over the hill, near Melton? You know? She's a bit tarty and he's not quite a gentleman."

"Oh yes, I remember."

'God you are awful Mum,' he thought. "Pass the grilled tomatoes please," he said.

"Good morning darling."

"Good morning my love. Hugs." How perfectly wonderful to see you".

This was his sister Molly, tall, ravishingly beautiful, long, flowing, lustrous, titian hair, wild and wonderful. They were besotted with each other. After almost scandalous embraces, she plonked down beside him. "Bacon and eggs and kidneys please, Charlotte, and coffee, lots please. Lots of coffee." Rough night, I'm afraid. Too much bubbly. The Cranbourne twins were back on leave from Felixtowe."

"Oh, from their small ships?"

32

"Yes, they ⁄spend their time dashing in and out of harbour in torpedo boats looking for trouble. They are always back by tea time though."

'Lucky chaps,' thought Cecil, thinking of his wet hole in the ground in France. He suddenly felt alone and lonely. This world was entirely too unreal. All the chatter. All the insignificance of it. This was not home any more. 'I've got to get out of here.' He touched his napkin to his mouth. "Er, I think I'll go for a walk."

"Want some company?"

"No thanks, Molly."

"I understand."

"Will you excuse me?" He looked around.

"What? what?" father spluttered, interrupting his concentration on the newspaper for a second to attack his egg again.

His mother barely looked up from her toast and marmalade. "That's right dear. A nice walk will do you good. I have a lot to do today, what with the vicar coming to tea and Mrs. Plunkett about the roses for the fair. Oh yes, I shall be as busy as can be."

Cecil collected his mack and cap and went outside. It was pleasant for an early spring day in northern England, brisk and fresh. He breathed in the clear air and with long strides paced down the road to the village, a mile or two over the hill. He thought, 'Alright I've got five more leave days. I don't think I want to stay here anymore. I'll go to Scotland and see Rowena and her father. Right. To the post office.'

After sending a telegram, he stopped at a pub in the village, one that they said was one of the oldest in England.

Second only to "The Trip To Jerusalem" in Nottingham, from where, they said, Crusaders began their journey to the Holy Land. After a couple of pints and a crusty thick slice of bread, cheese, and onion, he got up and started back up the hill to the house.

There was some disappointment from the family at his decision, but not as much as he had anticipated. The partings and absences had been so frequent in the recent past: first boarding school where his mother had been a rare visitor who kissed him once a year on visitors day, then the army with its forced and prolonged periods of family absences. continued the pattern of estrangement

Molly and Nigel were both sorry to see him go, but Father

only said something like, "Give the Hun one for me," and turned to his bugs and stamps again .His friendliness and vague hospitality of the day before now vanished. Mother was lying down with one of her headaches, her forehead covered with a silk hanky soaked in vinegar. She gave him a faint and distraught sigh, admonished him to be a good boy, and closed her eyes.

SCOTLAND AND ROWENA...

Cecil caught the Flying Scot that evening at Carlisle and was alighting at Stranraer that night.

"Hello my dear." It was a radiant Rowena, her eyes sparkling, smiling with pleasure after the brief time they had spent together on the train. Cecil was surprised at her warmth and the delightful, soft, and pliant way her lips and body felt against his.

"The car's over here," she said. They came to a large sports car with its top down. It looked like one of the new blown types and would be very fast. They growled out of the car park, the gears slipping into place like oiled jewellery, and roared up the hill, out of the town, and into the hills and moors of Wigtownshire. Rowena drove fast and with expertise, her hair streaming in the draft. It was too noisy to talk. They were silent but smiled at each other often. A gate came, she slowed and geared down, swung the great steering wheel around and followed a gravel drive that wound through trees which eventually came to the edge of a loch. She stopped the car and got out.

"Here we are. We go the rest of the way by boat." A small wooden craft lay rocking gently in the water. It was tied to a rickety-looking dock. She jumped nimbly down into it.

"Give me your bag." Cecil handed down his valise. She took it and stowed it under the low coaming that covered the forward part, under a dashboard on which there were a couple of instruments and a little steering wheel. She flicked a switch, pulled out the choke, and pressed a button. The engine coughed and smoked into life. "Let go that line Cecil."

He did as told and the boat, burbling and popping, moved away from the shore. It was pitch dark, but Cecil could see ahead some indistinct lights that flickered and blinked.

The boat was moving fairly fast now and cut through the water with a rippling sound.

"Ahoy there." The voice came from nearby.

"Hello," answered Rowena. She, very expertly, conned the boat neatly against a dock, and reversing the engine, came to a tidy stop, then cut the engine. She caught the line thrown through the air. The boat was made fast. All with no fuss or bother.

"Hello my boy." It was her father."

"Hello sir."

"Welcome to Balnagash."

It was now midnight and Cecil thought, 'Well I'm tired and that's why I'm seeing things,' for that was what he thought, looking up and seeing what looked like a castle looming above him. Well, not a castle, perhaps, more of a tower, a great, black, craggy tower, complete with arrow embrasures, crenellations, spires, and one gigantic iron-studded wooden door with steps of stone climbing to it. As he tottered up these, he noticed that father was wearing a kilt.

They entered a lofty room. The chief impression was grey stone, dim lighting, soft oriental rugs underfoot, and a smell of burning peat.

"Come and sit by the fire dear boy, and have a dram." He went to a large table that held a quantity of bottles, jugs, glasses, and soda. He poured out a measure and handed it to Cecil. "Try this. It's local."

Cecil sipped and sighed. "It's heavenly."

"Now, now, Daddy. He's exhausted."

"Well I am a bit, yes."

"Yes, of course. Off to bed. Not hungry?"

"No sir."

"Right. See you at breakfast."

"I'll show you your room Cecil. Come on." Rowena led him to where a flight of stone stairs wound upwards. Up two storeys and down a long dark hall.

"No electric up here." she said. "Just these candles. Here's your room."

"My God Rowena. It's more like a chamber. This is fantastic. A castle."

"Well, it's not really a castle, it's an old island fort. Not that old actually, 14th or 15th century, I think. It was meant to keep you Sassenachs out."

"Well, it seems pretty old to me."

"Alright darling. There's a hot water bottle in the bed. The bath and loo are in there. Brekkie at eight. I'll come and wake you with a kiss," she laughed in the most delightful way.

The silence was marvellous. Cecil slept, and his dreams

were sweet. He woke with sunshine beaming through a gap between the curtains. He turned and stretched. There was a knock at the door. "Come in."

The door swung open and Rowena came in with a cup of tea. "Sleep well?" she asked.

"Like a log. It was wonderful."

"Good. Hurry up and get dressed. Father's anxious to show you around and breakfast's ready in half an hour. By the way, here's the wake up I promised. She bent down and gave him a quite breathtaking kiss.

He couldn't help noticing that as she leaned down, rather more of her breasts were exposed than was proper for a young Edwardian girl. He gulped and said, "Er, yes, yes, of course, delighted, er, I'll be right down."

She pulled her gown together, blushing prettily.

After as quick a bath as possible, he dressed and practically ran down the steps. "Morning."

"Morning."

All the greetings were expressed. Breakfast of kippers, porridge, eggs, bacon, grilled tomatoes, toast, and Scotch marmalade were all consumed. Backs were leaned against chairs and cigarettes were lit. The general took a puff. "Ah, this is the life."

"It's a lovely day."

"Care for a walk around the island?"

"Love it."

"Right. Where's she gone? Ah here you are."

Rowena appeared, looking very fetching in a kilt and

heavy white pullover. She took Cecil's hand and led him out of the room, across the great hall, and through the open front door. The view was spectacular. The island was tiny, but beyond, the loch stretched as far as one could see, the hills rising above and forming an amphitheatre all around. The more distant hills had snow on them and were changing colours as the shadows formed by clouds sped by. The whole picture was made all the more heart wrenchingly beautiful by the sight and sound of gulls swooping and calling as they whirled around the tower.

They walked around to the other side of the building: on this part, the island was bigger and higher, a few small trees and some stunted bushes of gorse, otherwise, just close cropped turf, some heather, and a rock or two. A bleak, but pleasing prospect.

They walked about for a few minutes, when from one of the low hills ahead, a man appeared surrounded by sheep and a couple of sheep dogs. "Oh, there's Angus. Hello Angus," Rowena shouted.

"Hello to you. Good morning Laird.

"Morning Angus."

Introductions ensued. Cecil found himself looking at a tall, red-haired, bearded, handsome young man. His grip almost brought tears to Cecil's eyes. It was less of a handshake than a challenge, coupled as it was by a distinctly unfriendly glare.

'Oh, oh. Competition I think.' Some intermittent chat followed. Rather ratty looking animals had to be inspected and approved. The dogs sniffed suspiciously at Cecil's trews. It turned out that this was the general's prize collection, of which he was inordinately proud. Finally, the ceremony ended. Angus and sheep went one way, the others headed back to the house.

After lunch his host insisted on showing Cecil his stamp and insect collection, which even a non-philatelist and an entomologically limited person like Cecil could appreciate were impressive The general also showed him some notes he was working on for a book about military oddities. This was more interesting to Cecil, as military history was a passion of his. Some of the facts that the notes described were also quite new to him. The Royal Scots, the First of Foot, the oldest regiment in the British Army, were known as Pontius Pilate's body guard, tracing their lineage back to Hadrian's Legions. They had manned the wall lining the border between England and Scotland. Why the Royal Welsh Fusiliers wore a fan of black ribbon on the back of their tunics: commemorating an order to be allowed to retain this peculiarity that had been part of their uniform in the 1700s, relating to the little waxed wig they used to wear, because they had been at sea when the order came through to stop wearing wigs in the British Army. The Gloucester Regiment wore their cap badge (the Sphinx) front and back to remind one of their back-to-back stand against the enemy in Egypt. And on and on, the strangeness becoming more obscure and otiose as one dug deeper.

The next two days went so quickly as to be almost non-existent. The feeling of fondness for each other had grown so that by the time the last evening had arrived, they were besotted with each other. Angus had not made another appearance, to Cecil's relief, and father had retired to his study, so they had all the privacy they needed to gaze at each other and hold hands as they went for walks in this magical place.

As Cecil lay in the darkness of his room that night, trying to collect his thoughts, for tomorrow he left at dawn's crack for the south and the boat to France, he reflected on the past week's occurrences. It had all been quite overwhelming, happy, but confusing. Still, basically, a teenager, this was all grown-up stuff. He sighed. 'Oh well. To sleep.' He turned over and buried his head in the pillow. At that moment, the door opened.

"Oh my dear." He felt her sweet breath as she whispered. He felt her body as she slipped off her gown. She was quite naked. She put her arms around his neck and gently pulled him down as she lay beneath him. Though totally without experience, he tried not to be too clumsy.

She said, "It's alright my darling."

He felt her stroking and her kissing and, oh God, her warmth and soft moistness. Oh god, oh God... . Yes, yes.

They lay like children, loving and sleeping, cuddled in each others arms for the rest of the night.

Dawn came too soon, as she slipped out of the bed.

"Must go sweet, before Daddy gets up."

Breakfast and packing and leave-taking took place. So perfunctory. So matter of fact. So bloody awful.

They parted at the station. They were going to London down the west coast. Cecil was going via the east to Dover for the boat to France.

    Somehow the day passed. Although he was elated at his new love, the pit of his stomach was full of sadness and apprehension. It had all seemed so magical, and now was over. So fleeting. He thought of what waited ahead and shivered.

BACK AT THE FRONT...

The boat crossing was rough and he was relieved when Calais was reached, even though in rain. Onto the train crowded with troops chattering and laughing about their leaves. The train stopped at Albert, where he got off and sought transport to the area just behind where his battalion was.

It was late afternoon, when trudging ahead of a small number of soldiers who were also going to his sector, he saw the flickering lights that marked the front. The sky was rapidly darkening as low, grey, ragged clouds scudded across the horizon. They were now crossing a shell-hole-pocked field. A figure detached itself from a shelter.

"Scots Fusiliers?"

"Yes," answered Cecil.

"Right this way sir. I'm the guide. Follow me. Here's the steps down." They were now half crouching in a communication trench which wound its way to the support and front line and which they negotiated. The nearer they got to their destination, the more downcast Cecil became.

Crash. Thud. Crash. Thud. A couple of mortar rounds exploded over to their right. 'Christ,' thought Cecil, 'Welcome home.'

" 'Ere we are sir. HQ's down that way."

"Thank you."

"Oh blimey. Look what the cat dragged in. How are you dear boy?" This was Bobbety Robertson.

"Oh, hello chaps. How wonderful to be back I don't think. What's the news."

"Oh, the usual. The balloon's going up next week. You're just in time.

"Bugger. I was hoping I'd miss it."

"Don't let his nibs hear you talk like that."

"No." He passed his hand over his face wearily. "Anything to drink?"

"Of course. get a drink for Mr. Paynter, Billings. Want something to eat?"

"No. I had dinner in Albert."

The next few days went by in a frenzy of preparation. They were on a relatively quiet part of the line, so that apart from the usual early morning 'hate', things were fairly livable. The concentration was all on getting ready to move to the south, to the area astride the River Somme where the upcoming offensive was to take place.

The big day arrived. The whole regiment was fallen in on the road to Albert, where trains waited to take them the rest of the way.

"Attention! In fours. Left turn! By the right. Quick march!"

They swung off down the road, the officer commanding

and the adjutant on horseback, leading, then the pipes and drums, the rest in their companies following, Cecil leading his platoon. This was the part he liked the best: the pipes and drums going full tilt, the men swinging side by side, the boots going crunch, crunch, the equipment jingling and slapping, making a rhythmic background to the chief instruments.

Arrival was accomplished and the whole marshalling process was repeated, only backwards. The trenches they were to occupy had been held before by the French and were quite deep and quite tidy, which was as pleasant a surprise as it was unusual, French trenches not having a reputation for being in the best of shape as a rule.

Saturday, July 1st. 7:30 a.m. 72 degrees. Clear sky.

With the Manchester Regiment on their left and the Green Howards on their right, they clambered out of their trenches. Whistles were screeching up and down the lines, and bagpipes groaning and creaking as pipers blew and squeezed and then getting into their stride with "The Black Bear." Cecil, walking stick in one hand, revolver in the other, picked his way through and around barbed wire entanglements. Leaning forward for balance, he glanced to his right. 'Good.' There was the trusty company sergeant major looking fierce and determined. 'Good man.' To his left, and slightly ahead, the piper was giving as good a tune as if on parade. Artillery rounds were slicing overhead without pause. The noise, indescribable, but comforting. This was their barrage and was dropping just ahead of them like a curtain. The ground ahead seemed to be boiling, flashing, crashing, and disintegrating. A quick look back. A line of glinting steel: the bayonets of his men. Yelling and crowding behind him..

Suddenly they were at the edge of the German trenches. They were virtually empty except for some ragged looking inert bodies and some, with their hands up, shouting to be spared. The trenches were all fallen in. The guns had done their work.

Cecil stood for a moment or two leaning against the trench side, panting with the efforts he had just been through. After taking stock with his sergeant, he climbed a ladder that leaned against the back of the trench and looked around. The barrage continued on, but seemed less heavy than before. There were some troops ahead spreading out. Looking back he could see reinforcements coming up. 'Probably the Bedfords,' he thought. 'Right. Our job's ahead. Trones Wood.' He quickly checked his map.

"Right Sar'nt. Off we go. Get the men going."

"Right you are sir."

"Alright. On your feet lads. .

This time they were not to be let off as lightly as the first time. The Germans were ready for them now and opened up with a vengeance, the chalky ground sending up great clouds of dust with every explosion. The ground was really churned up now, shell holes everywhere. Added to the general pandemonium was the ominous rat-tat-tat of machine guns. The fire was coming from ahead and from the left. This was causing the troops to move away and to their right, a tendency that Cecil tried to prevent by forcing himself to go towards the gunfire, hoping it would set the right example.

But at that split second disaster struck. the piper was hit and went down on his knees. Cecil, as he turned to help him, felt a piercing pain in his ankle. 'Christ Almighty, that hurt.' He fell dropping his stick and revolver. He was aware of someone shouting.

"Stretcher bearers. Mr. Paynter's been hit." Then he passed out. He was dreaming. He was flying over water and mountains. He was leaping in big strides over buildings, floating, someone was crying, moaning, weeping.

"Hello. Hello." He came to with a start. The noise was like someone blubbering, crying. 'No it was a bubbling sound. Where? What is it?' It was dark except for intermittent flashing from somewhere. Then, with a hissing roar, a rocket illuminated the surrounding area with brilliant white light. He realized who and where he was. He ached all over and there was a dull throbbing pain in his left leg. It all came back . As the flare died down, he saw that he was in a shell hole and the crying noise was coming from a figure at his side.

He fumbled for a match which flickered on briefly. The other occupant of the hole was a German. He felt for his Webley. 'Damn.' Of course he'd dropped it. 'Oh well. This chap didn't look too dangerous.' Another flare. It gave enough light to see that his companion had just expired. Sightless eyes gazed at eternity.

Cecil tried to sit up and look around, but the pain was too excruciating. He fell back trembling. He managed to find a small piece of chocolate and munched on that. A swig from his water bottle. 'Thank God! A fag.' He lit the cigarette and felt better. 'Alright. No panic. Try to relax. Someone will find me in the morning. Let's hope it's not a bloody German.' He managed to fall asleep.

Gradually coming to after the long night, Cecil was aware of dawn, not from the sun, but by cold raindrops falling. 'Oh God. That's all I need.' He tried to move and was just able to support himself on his right elbow. He could just see over the lip of the hole.

"Hello. Stretcher bearer," he called. It came out as a weak croak, but, blessed be the angels, he heard nearby and behind, a shout.

" 'Allo, 'allo."

A figure came towards him.' Thank the Lord, it had a red cross armlet on. Help was at hand!'

"Oy. Bill. There's an officer down 'ere."

"Alright sir. We'll look after you. 'Ere. Gently now."

They helped him carefully onto the stretcher. Whiz, bang crash! A shell splashed into a hole nearby and showered them in dirt.

"Christ. That was a near one."

He was conscious of the men crouching over him as if to protect him. These were brave men, unarmed, noncombatant, but in the thick of it. Some of them were conscientious objectors, some were Quakers, just averse to killing their fellow man. All were brave.

Half walking, half stumbling, always with their shoulders

hunched forward, they managed to cross the ground back to the old British lines. Shells were crumping down all around, but they were out of range of musketry. At last he was placed on the ground with other wounded and injured men.

He raised himself up on one elbow and looked around. One of the stretcher bearers said,

"There you go sir. Good luck. A doctor will be along directly."

"Thank you. All of you." He looked directly at one of the bearers who happened to be a German soldier prisoner who looked at him blankly through small round glasses. Cecil lay back down and closed his eyes.

"Hello old man. How are you feeling?"

Cecil opened his eyes. A spectacled man in a soiled, bloody, white smock leaned over him.

"Not too bad, thank you doc."

"Let's see. Ah, that's a good one. Nice and clean. Went right through. It's Blighty for you alright. Orderly get this officer on the ambulance for advanced dressing."

CLEAN SHEETS...

After what seemed an eternity of bumping, rattling movement, accompanied by groans and curses, the ambulance finally reached a collection of tents and huts. The orderlies unloaded the wounded and carried them inside one of the huts. It was bright and warm inside and smelled of iodine and alcohol.

Cecil felt himself being laid on a bed, a real bed, with sheets, white sheets, clean and crisp, a pillow under his head. 'Oh blessed Heaven. What comfort. What joy.'

"Hello. I'm your nurse. My name's Susan."

He opened his eyes and really thought himself in Heaven. A pretty young woman in the starched uniform of a Sister of the Canadian Army Nursing Service stood there smiling.

Thus began the day that changed his life. They say you always fall in love with the nurse, but it's not always that the nurse falls for you. Here was the exception.

Over the next few days that Cecil lay there, virtually helpless, Susan tended his wounds, fed him, washed him, talked to him, and listened to him. And while the every-day work went on, their affection for each other grew. Susan would tell him of her life in Canada. She lived on a farm in Alberta which sounded like heaven to Cecil. She described the rolling foothills and the majesty of the mountains, the openness of the people, and the general lack of class differences.

There was a period every day when dressings were attended to or when medications were administered, that they could spend time together. The ward he was in wasn't large and there were just four other patients in it. They all shared Susan and another nurse, a girl from Yorkshire who knew of Susan's and Cecil's attachment, and who would keep the other's attention. Cecil watched Susan's face while she talked about the hills and forests and lakes of her beloved Canada.

Susan was fair with deep blue eyes. She would speak of her father and mother who were both of Scottish origin. Cecil would wince a little, inside, thinking of Rowena and his love for her, and he wondered and worried, but Susan was here and Rowena was far away, and he was young and this was now. 'Oh God, what can I do?' He turned his attention to Susan who was now talking of her brothers, both at the front and for whom she worried every day. She told him of her plans to go back to school to study medicine and hopefully become a doctor when the war was over.

Cecil's wound apparently was not serious. The bullet from a machine gun had penetrated the soft part of the ankle below the bone and had passed cleanly through, exiting out the other side. He was to be sent home to recuperate and would probably be returned to the front in a matter of weeks.

The other patients were not so lucky though. They would most likely recover, but they had facial traumas and would be disfigured badly. When they were through here they were to be sent to a hospital in England that was becoming famous for its cosmetic surgical work and that would reconstruct, as far as was possible, the dreadful damage that had been done.

Because the ward was fairly small, any inclinations between Cecil and Susan other than verbal, had to be tempered with some circumspection. They were both commissioned officers and had to play the game. But in little ways, and day by day, their feelings for each other became more difficult to hide, so that by the end of the week, Cecil's fellow patients began to make the usual ribald comments.

On the day before he was to be sent to England for further treatment, leave, and recuperation, Susan came to carry out routine matters as usual, checking dressings, temperatures, and so on. She was downcast. She knew he was leaving next day. Cecil tried to reassure her and express his love for her as passionately as he could.

She, being rather more practical than he, pointed out the dangers ahead, the chances of their being together in the immediate future were slight indeed. He would be returned to the trenches when fit. Her whereabouts were altogether in the lap of other superiors. She could be sent anywhere in France or Flanders, and when the war was over, what then? She would return to Canada and her life there; he to England and what awaited him. They promised to write when they could. He knew the hospital he was being sent to in England, as did she. He hoped she would keep her promise.

The next day Cecil made his goodbyes to the others.

Good wishes and general badinage ensued. Promises of undying friendships were made lightly and without much belief. Odds were pretty good that most of them would get the chop before too long.

He limped to the door where an orderly stood with Susan.

"Corporal Jones here will look after you Sir," she said formally, batting her eyes at the same time.

"Thank you nurse, for all your care ." She had her cloak on, so as he stood there, he discreetly took hold of her hand and squeezed gently beneath its cover.

"Au revoir my darling," he whispered.

She nodded and squeezed back. Turning to hide his tears he moved over to where the ambulance stood.

RECUPERATING...

There are many unpleasant things in life. Short of sheer physical pain and the possibility of imminent demise, seasickness is there among the leaders. Loneliness, hopelessness ,for one reason or another, the list goes on, but high on the list must come separation from one's loved ones, especially when love is new and parting is obligatory. The gloom, the melancholy, the utter torment.

Cecil, suffering all these manifestations, gazed at the passing fields of France. It was raining, and prospects were depressing in the extreme. He was sharing the compartment with other walking wounded, who were all in high spirits, playing cards, laughing, drinking scotch from the bottle, and generally having the time of their lives.

"How about a game Paynter?" a captain of engineers asked.

"Come on. Smithers is too drunk. He's useless."

"What are the stakes?"

"Five bob a bet."

"Oh alright. Give us a swig."

The bottle was passed to him. He took a deep swallow. It burnt wonderfully going down.

"Ah, that's better. Anyone got a cig?' Someone threw

him a Players. Someone else lit it.

"Right. Deal away."

Some four hours later the train rattled into a station. Boulogne had been reached. Doors slammed up and down the line with much shouting and cursing. Everyone tried to get out at once. Manhandling luggage, porters struggled to help.

Finally, Cecil was on the platform looking about for directions. At the gate, red-capped military police stood, officious, as always, checking papers, grim and watchful, looking out for the possible deserters.

Cecil passed all these and made his way to the gangway that angled up to the steam packet that lay alongside the pier, and which, at precisely nine p.m., would convey him and all this eager, damp, tired collection of military humanity to another world that was collectively known as Blighty.

In the bar, which he made for as soon as he got aboard, his erstwhile companions of the train were already settled with their cards. The stewards were busily scurrying back and forth with brandy, scotch, soda siphons, and what appeared to be ham sandwiches. 'Ah, that's what I need.'

He gave his order and soon was munching away as he looked dolefully at his cards. Needless to say, once the vessel had got to port in England, he was flat broke and had a slight hangover.

He slept fitfully in the train to London and was asleep when they got to Charing Cross.

"Wake up Paynter." It was one of his new chums from the game, a lieutenant of Irish Guards who had also offered to put him up at his house in town, until Cecil had been to the bank and replenished funds.

"Oh, thanks Gerald. With you in a sec."

A taxi was requisitioned and soon they were bowling along Piccadilly to the area known as Belgravia. 'Crikey,' thought Cecil. 'This chap's got money.'

"Here we are driver. Number seventeen."

They pulled up at a house on a terraced street. It was quite late now, but the light was on above the front door and there was a light in one of the windows on the ground floor. The cab was paid off and they went up the steps.

The door was black and shiny with a large knocker in brass shaped like an Irish harp. Gerald lifted it and gave a couple of bangs. The door opened almost at once. An elderly butler in black fustian said,

"Good evening master Gerald."

"Evening Mathews. Pater in?"

"Yes sir. The general has retired for the evening."

"Oh, right. This is Mr. Paynter. He will be staying for a night or two. Bring us some sandwiches would you? In the drawing room I think."

They gave their greatcoats to the servant along with caps and canes. Gerald led the way into a room of some magnificence.

"Sit down by the fire old man. I'll make some drinks. Whiskey alright?"

Bloody alright," answered Cecil.

"I'm sorry father's not still up. You'll like him. He's as dotty as can be since mother died ,but he's alright."

"Did the butler say 'general' ?" Asked Cecil.

"Yes, the old duffer was pretty senior. Did some good work in India and the Sudan with Kitchener. Finished up commanding a division in South Africa. He was in this lot in '14, then invalided out. Still misses it though."

Morning came too soon. Cecil woke with a crashing hangover. He looked blearily for his watch and saw the time. Ten a.m. 'Got to get up and get to the bank.' He did that, after consuming a couple of boiled eggs, toast, and scalding hot coffee, served by the retainer of last night, who advised him that master Gerald would not arise until noon, On the heels of this announcement, entered a small, irascible-looking elderly gentleman, dressed as though for a formal function. Morning-coated and boutonnièred. Grey topper in one hand, gold knobbed stick in the other.

"Who the hell are you?" he sputtered. "One of that young idiot's fast friends I suppose. Well it's no good his asking for more money. I don't know what you idle wasters do with it all over there anyway. There's nothing to spend it on I'm sure. There certainly wasn't in South Africa. Well eat your breakfast and then clear off!"

"But I'm not what you think I am."

"What, what? Well explain yourself."

Cecil did so, in spades.

"Well, I apologise. But really. No wonder I'm in such a state. We are supposed to be at the Palace in an hour for the Levee. Did you know he's getting an MC today?"

I didn't know. I'll get him up." Cecil ran up the stairs and opened the door to Gerald's room.

"Come on. Up you get." He went to the window and pulled the heavy curtains apart. The sunshine poured in.

"Jesus Christ." A muffled voice came from under tumbled sheets. "What the hell. Bugger off. I'm sleeping.

"No you're not. You're going to Buck House to see the King."

"Oh God! I forgot. Where's my stuff?"

"All here. Nice and shiny." The dress uniform, scarlet tunic, gold-braided, the buttons in fours befitting the Irish Regiment of Foot Guards, the trousers red striped: all neatly hung on the back of a chair. Black bearskin helmet with pale blue hackle on a separate stand of its own. In short order Gerald was being helped into a cab and off to get his medal.

The father, rushing past Cecil, said,

"I won't forget this. Let me know if there is anything I can do for you. Anytime. Very grateful." Cecil would have good reason to remember this promise in the weeks to come.

Repairs of a financial nature were undertaken at his bank for funds to be distributed to everyone's satisfaction.

Cecil walked out of the building with that light springy step that one acquires when leaving an institution of monetary storage with cash in one's pocket.

That afternoon he was on his way home and arrived at the station, to be met, as usual, by Nigel, with the words,

"Christ Almighty. Shot through the ankle. What were you doing? Walking on your fucking hands?"

Cecil rested and recuperated for two weeks at the hospital, which was just north of London and where he found, to his delight, a letter from Susan, waiting for him. The news was fantastic. She was going to get a week's leave and spend it in Paris. Could he join her? He quickly made some calculations and wrote her back to say that he could: the last few days after he was released from hospital and before he went back to the front, were free.

An examination pronounced him fit for return to France, and the following week saw him on the boat to Calais where he got on the train to Paris. He had splurged and was traveling first class. As he sat in the dining saloon sipping on a brandy and soda, he gazed across the jetty where another train stood raising steam. This one was not going to Paris. It was a leave train returning troops to the trenches. He shivered. In just a few days this would be him. He was going directly to the lines from Paris.

Cecil had told Susan when and where he was arriving, but had not got an answer before he left London, so he was hoping she would just be at the station to meet him. As the train rattled through the early evening gloom, he sat thinking, looking out into the gathering darkness, puffing on a Player's cigarette and savouring his brandy, when suddenly, on the distant east horizon he saw a glare of light, indistinct and flickering. Someone in the carriage, a woman, said, *"Pauvre poilus."* He swallowed his drink and tried to sleep.

PARIS...

The sound of much hooting and chatter and bustle, and many lights woke him. The train was arriving at the *Gare du Nord*. He began to gather his belongings. He lowered the window, letting in the smoky, damp, outside air, and sniffed. The platform came in sight and he looked for Susan.

The platform was packed with people, mostly soldiers, mostly French, in their distinctive horizon-blue uniforms and Adrian Helmet, a sprinkling of Legionnaires from North Africa easily identifiable in their white kepis.

The train came slowly to a grumbling, clanking, wheezing stop. He climbed down onto the step and to the pavement and looked around at the utter confusion all about him. Where was she? Would she be there?

He put his shoulder down and literally fought his way to the terminus. It was only when he reached the gate where tickets were collected that he realised that people waiting to meet the train weren't allowed past the railings.

Then he thought he was going to faint. There she was! Laughing, beautiful, her wonderful red hair tumbling about her sweet face. She rushed into his arms crying with joy. They both started to talk at once. Kissing, tears fell like rain on his cheeks and felt like champagne. It was all too utterly marvellous for words.

"Well," said Cecil, "it's so absolutely bloody wonderful to see you. Let's get a cab and get out of this pandemonium."

"We don't have to my darling," said Susan smiling. "I've rented a small flat. It's just around the corner from here, a teeny walk."

"Wonderful. Show me the way."

It was, as Susan had said, a small flat. It was in fact minuscule, but it was charming and cozy. It had a glassed studio-style skylight. An artist had lived there before the war. All the furniture had been left when he'd gone to the front. There was a small fireplace. Susan knelt down to light it and a crackling blaze was soon going.

They had stopped at a market on the way and bought some cold meat, some cheese, bread, tomatoes, and a couple of bottles of claret. Cecil removed the cork from one of them and poured two glasses, one of which he handed to Susan. They clinked and looked into each other's eyes. Hers were still shining with tears.

"Oh God. I'm sorry. I can't stop crying. I'm so happy."

Cecil put his glass down and took her in his arms.

"My love," he said hoarsely. "Let's drink and eat later. Now I just want to hold you and to love you."

He woke. The darkness was profound. He looked at her. She was asleep, her breath, sibilant and soft. He looked at his watch. Midnight. 'Got to get up and pee,' he thought. On the way to the little toilet he stopped and looked out of the skylight. The moon seemed fitful in a sky full of scudding clouds. It had rained a little. The roof shone. It was as though he was looking through tears. He certainly felt like crying. It was all too beautiful and too brief. Just a couple of days left.

He heard a rustle behind him. It was Susan. She came up to him and held him around his waist from behind. She pressed her head to his back and squeezed. "Ouch." He flinched.

"What? What is it darling?"

"I need to pee." They separated, laughing. He ran to the small room. 'Just in time!' She was still laughing when he got back. They laughed and loved themselves back to their dreams.

They spent the next morning, first in a little café round the corner, full of brass things, mirrored walls, and palms in buckets. An old man in black with a long apron served them croissants and cafe au lait. Then they explored until they were dropping with exhaustion.

A funny old cab, with driver even older, hunched but cheerful, drove them, hooting through crowded streets to their little paradise. He saluted Cecil with a *"Bon Chance Mon Brave."* Cecil heaped francs into his horny old hand.

They made love and slept until dark, then to the same cafe for a dinner of French country cooking, the whole feast accompanied with some first class Bordeaux. Then coffee in tiny cups. When they got back, they were almost too tired to make love, but managed somehow.

He heard her cry in the night.

Next morning came the day they had dreaded. Susan had a few more days leave left and was going to the south to look around before going back to her hospital. For Cecil though, no such luck. He had to catch a train at ten that would take him to Amiens and then by lorry and foot to the lines.

Susan helped him pack his few belongings and went with him to the station. She clung to him. All the time there was a sort of desperation about all she did. She stared at him and hung onto his arm. All her movements were nervous and quick. She seemed apprehensive and intense, unlike her usual sweet, funny, vagueness that he loved so much.

He bought some magazines and cigarettes. They found his platform where the train waited. An enormous black locomotive was at the head. The area was full of troops, mostly French.

Cecil found an empty compartment and opened the door. He turned to Susan who was now weeping uncontrollably.

"Don't my sweet. It will be alright. We will stay in touch and we will marry as soon as this nonsense is over."

"Oh darling. I wish I could believe that. I just can't see it happening. I have to go back to Canada. You will go back to your life in England and forget all about me."

"No, that's not going to happen. I'll find you somehow."

The engine gave its funny little French toot.

"Alright, big kiss, big hug." Cecil tried to be gently lighthearted. It didn't really work. They kissed passionately.

"Goodbye my love." He climbed into the carriage and shut the door, opened the window, and hung out to hold her hands. She looked deeply into his eyes.

"Be safe, my dearest, my love forever."

"My love to you sweetest Susan."

The train jerked and began to move. They let go of each others hands. She blew kisses. He waved and kissed back. The train increased speed. She became indistinct then disappeared in the crowd. He turned and sat down, his head in his hands, and wept.

BACK AT THE FRONT...

The blessings of sleep blotted out his misery for a while, so that by the time he awoke they had almost reached their destination, Amiens. Everyone detrained.

Too soon, he was trudging down the old, familiar puddled, mud road that led through Albert to the collection area at the eastern edge of the broken, battered city.

"Any transport for the 19th div area?" 'Why was it always late in the day that he arrived back at the front? And why was the sky always that poisonous colour?' It was yellow from the setting sun low down on the western horizon, but a yellow unlike any he had ever seen on an artist's palette, a colour that rejected any familiarity with warmth or joy, just a sullen forlorn announcement that the day was ending – with the inevitable, scudding, grey clouds moving across the sky, and that it was going to be a wet, cold, unpleasant night.

He found his way to his dugout and was greeted with the usual ribaldry. Somehow though, it seemed less lively. Even Bobbety was quieter than usual.

It was autumn of 1916 now. Most of them had been out since the winter. The strain was beginning to tell.

"Tea sir?" It was their trusty batman who never seemed to change, and always was able to produce a decent cup of tea whatever the circumstances.

The men in the battalion seemed to be mostly reliable and dependable. They were lads from the farms, some from the coal pits, a few clerks, some ship-builders, some fisher folk. Strong, on the short side, plucky and uncomplaining. They were, in their outlook, fair-minded, quite conservative, and very Presbyterian. Just a few RCs from the islands, but mostly non-conformist.

Days merged into each other and disappeared unmourned. It was a cold, winter, stormy, and inflexible, the ground, like iron, the sky like steel. The protagonists left each other virtually alone. Christmas came with the Catholic Bavarians opposite singing carols with a brilliance and beauty that broke many a Protestant heart. The regiment stood above the parapet and applauded, firing flares carefully above heads, in an attempt at some kind of seasonal display.

Nineteen seventeen came, and with it the offensives that the powers that be, had concocted over winter: the campaigns and battles around Arras. Vimy Ridge was taken with individualistic Canadian aplomb and guts.

The tank had been introduced earlier on the Somme, but was used latterly with more success at Cambrai and was receiving great praise and plaudits as a war-winning device.

Then came the excessive horrors of Third Ypres and Paschendaele.

Cecil had received several letters from Rowena, all written in the most affectionate, warm manner. He had not had one word from Susan. He wondered and worried about that, and about what lay ahead. She had not given him an address. As she was being moved about, she had promised to write when settled.

"Paynter, you down there?" It was the peculiarly growly voice of the adjutant.

"Yes sir. Just having a rest. Off duty, you know."

Adjutants are the second in command to officers commanding battalions, and are often hard-bitten abrasive types. This was no exception. Though Cecil was off duty, he stiffened to attention, feeling guilty to have been caught lying down.

"Right, right. As you were. Stand easy. We don't know what sort of influences you have or what particular angel you have looking over your shoulder, but we've received orders from above that you're seconded to staff HQ as of now. Pack your bags and be off with you. Travel papers and other instructions will be ready in an hour. You can take your servant with you, if you like. Right. Carry on."

As he turned on his heel to climb the stairs, he grunted:

"Lucky bastard."

Of course Cecil knew what this was all about. Rowena's father pulling strings. Damn. Though elated at the chance to get out of this hellhole, he felt the guilt of being unduly favoured by the accident of circumstances. This feeling lasted about two seconds. 'The hell with it. Better lucky than clever.' He called for his man who was new to him. His name was Johnson.

"We're going to a better hole Johnson." He explained the

situation.

"Come on. Let's have a quick one together to celebrate." Here they were then, clinking grimy jam jars half full of whisky.

"Good luck to us both sir," said the beaming corporal.

"Amen." said Cecil.

"Welcome to Headquarters," a captain, black buttoned and badged indicating a rifle regiment said, with hand extended.

"Corporal, take Mr. Paynter's servant round the back and show him the ropes. He looks hungry too."

"Right. Come in my dear chap .My names Adair" He led Cecil into a great room, heavily curtained, lavishly carpeted with walls panelled and mirrored. What were obviously antiques of some magnificence furnished the room. A fire blazed at one end where some divans and chairs were drawn up. A low hum of conversation buzzed, music played on a gramophone in one corner, the scent of tobacco prevailed. Altogether an atmosphere far from that of the cold and mud and danger of the front line that he had just left. Cecil thought he was in heaven.

"Alright chaps. Introductions all round. New man straight from up there." He nodded in the general direction of the east.

"Good. Get him a drink first."

Everyone crowded round to shake hands and say a few words. In his soiled uniform, he felt uncomfortably out of place. Most of the officers here were in the uniform of one of the Guard's regiments: a couple of riflemen and a highlander in kilt. They all, however, looked exceedingly well pressed and very clean.

"Any chance of a hot bath sir?"

"Of course, dear boy. What can I have been thinking? Steward, take Mr. Paynter up to his room and show him the bathroom. Dinner's at eight. We don't dress."

His room was quite astounding, panelled in white and gold and furnished in *Louis Quinze*. Spectacular actually. And thinking of where he had been that morning, slightly obscene. 'Oh well. Where's the bath?'

Dinner was simple but elegant. By comparison to the rations up front, it was positively sumptuous. He slept the sleep of kings that night. No nightmares which had been visiting him more frequently lately, to his dismay.

His batman woke him with a cup of tea and a bowl of hot water for shaving.

"Are you being looked after alright Thompson?"

"Yessir. I'm well quartered, very comfy. Breakfast is being served in short order sir."

"Right. Thank you. Carry on."

Breakfast was pleasant, but abbreviated. No one hung about. They ate and disappeared to their various duties.

"When you are ready Paynter." It was the rifleman who had initially greeted him!

"Take you to your office and show you your tasks for the day."

Cecil's main job apparently, was to assist the adjutant

with his duties: mostly extra paperwork, so he was in effect a glorified clerk, but the afternoons were virtually his own. He spent them reading a little book of poetry that Rowena had given him, and walking through the unspoilt countryside of this part of Picardy, gentle rolling country that reminded him of parts of England's midlands.

The headquarters that he was attached to were part of a division that was in the 5th Army, commanded by a general whose name was Hubert Gough. He was an Ulsterman, an ex-cavalry officer and a thruster. He was not particularly liked by his peers or his men. He had a reputation for bad luck and soldiers were not happy if they were transferred to his command.

Unfortunately for Cecil and his HQ, a well-planned and well-executed German attack of major proportions was about to fall on their part of the line, and although they were some twelve miles behind the front, the German assault troops reached the village just a couple of miles down the road very quickly and on the Friday of that week. Retreating British troops began to pass by the Chateau, first in some order, then in straggling groups, lost and forlorn, telling of disaster, and that they were the last of such-and-such a regiment, only to be to be told to fall in up the road with the remainder of the last survivors of such-and-such regiment.

Orders had come down to evacuate the Chateau and papers were being burned in the garden. Cecil was, to his dismay, made officer in charge of the rearguard. He was helped by a grizzled old company sergeant major who got a rag-tag group together: clerks and cooks mostly, none familiar with a rifle, and he had them fall in on the lawn for Cecil's inspection. Cecil's heart fell when he saw them.

"Well let's do what we can. Now everyone except for us are going that way," he nodded towards the west. "We, on the other hand, will go this way," (pointing towards the village and the east).

"Sar'nt Major."

"Sah!"

"Get the men into extended order. You take the left flank, I'll be in the centre, and you corporal," he addressed a thin, little man with a very white face who had served him drinks in the bar last week, "you look after the right end, alright?"

"Right sir." said the corporal, getting, if possible, even paler.

"Right. Off we go. Open order. Shoot at anything wearing a grey uniform. You all have enough ammo for a while. There will be no more, so be a bit careful about waste. Right, off we go."

They all scattered until they were in a long strung-out line and began to move forward. They seemed surprisingly adept at what they were doing, bobbing about, keeping low.

They reached the crossroads near the village, which is when they first saw their enemy, a column of German troops moving at the double, officers leading, but with no scouts out ahead.

Cecil couldn't believe his luck. He could see his sergeant

look at him enquiringly. Cecil waved and shouted.

"Open fire. Five rounds rapid, then fix bayonets." A volley of mostly inaccurate shots rang out. Not many Germans fell, but the surprise was complete. By the time bayonets were clumsily fixed, the Germans had fallen back in disarray. Both officers were down Cecil noticed.

He blew his whistle and croaked out of a dry throat a sound that might have sounded like "Charge." He jumped up from where he had been crouching and leaped across a ditch onto the road. The men followed him, yelling for all they were worth. The Germans, who must have been raw recruits by the way they behaved, broke and ran. Cecil's men fired one shattering volley after them.

Cecil blew his whistle again, signaling to the NCOs to regroup, which they did, and Cecil quickly congratulated them and said,

"Right. Lets be off. That last bit will keep them back for a while. Form fours. 'Tenshun. By the right, double march." They trotted back to where Cecil reckoned the official rearguard would be.

Some hours later, puffing and sweating, clattering down a small hill, they saw ahead a barrier of tree branches and over-turned carts blocking the road, held by a small group of British troops.

"Where the fuck did you lot come from?"

"Oh, beg pardon sir. Didn't see an officer." A red-faced NCO saluted.

"That's alright sergeant. We are HQ's rear guard."

"Yessir. Keep up this road. It's under fire sir. Keep your heads down."

Cecil eventually found his group and reported the happenings of the day.

"Well done Paynter. This will mean an MC at least." remarked his commanding officer.

"Thank you sir. I think we all rather enjoyed it."

"Good, good. Well, carry on."

The German offensive continued with varying amounts of success, but the British, Dominion, and French Armies were able to sustain themselves, and maintained a steady and remorseless defence which in the end wore down the fighting will of the enemy forces. The German offensive faltered and petered out. The Allied offensive began. When the end finally came, Cecil was back with his battalion having been returned to the fighting line along with many others like him who were needed to help stem the onslaught.

Then the word came through at eleven a.m. on the eleventh of November to cease fire and stand down. There had been intermittent firing right up until that time, so that when it ended the silence was almost unnerving. Then with a stutter a German machine gun opposite went rat-tat-a-tat-tat... tat-tat. The rounds were fired well over their heads. The German soldier firing, stood up, took off his helmet, and bowed towards the British lines, straightened up, saluted, turned, and walked away. Cecil's company jumped on top of the parapet and cheered. Cecil knew that the German troops opposite were the friendly Saxons they had met before, so often.

Later that day, Cecil found three of his brother officers, and with a bottle of Johnny Walker and a pack of cards they got into the deepest dugout they could find and played bridge for the rest of the day, their enjoyment spoiled only by the irritating sound of an American artillery battery up top trying to be the last unit to fire a shot in the war.

DEMOBILIZATION...

"Wake up dearie."

Susan slowly came out of her dreams which had been golden, surreal, and wonderful. She wearily dragged herself back to reality. 'Where was she? Oh, I know. I'm on my way home.'

The train rattled and swayed. She wiped the misted window with her cuff. Someone had been playing noughts and crosses, the 'x's had won. She rubbed vigorously and peered out through the grimy window.

The countryside was a greyish green. The trees, smudged and indistinct, lined the horizon. It was raining lightly and looked utterly depressing. Typical north French countryside in winter.

Yesterday she had said goodbye to fellow nurses and some of the doctors. The armistice had been signed. The guns were silent. Mankind was friends again. The train she was on was taking her to Calais, to the ferry that would sail her to England, where she would, eventually, board a ship for Canada. She shivered with pleasure at the thought. Perhaps she might be home in less than a month. Home for spring. Home with her family and friends. Home. And yet... her heart sank, she thought of Cecil. Where he might be. Whether he was still alive. The letters had stopped.

The days and weeks since she had seen him in Paris and spent that wonderful week had dragged interminably. The whole episode now seemed like dream. Though she looked forward to going, her life now would never be quite complete. She knew this as a fact. Whatever lay ahead, life was not to be wholly happy ever again.

For Cecil. the next few months passed slowly and uneventfully. He had to report to the regimental depot which was in the town of Ayr in western Scotland. The interminable process of demobilisation took place, the whole business dealt with in typical civil service manner, soullessly, and without compassion. One moment one was a soldier of the King, serving a grateful nation and government, the next, out on the street without a job, prospects, or chums. And the last was the hardest to bear.

Cecil would discover how important camaraderie had been and how he would miss it. He considered his immediate future. He really had no prospects. Perhaps he should contact Gerald, who might put him up. Then get in touch with Rowena and her father. He wanted to thank him for the staff job he was sure the old man had got for him.

His feelings for Rowena were mixed. He was fond of her, but unsure of anything stronger. His really deep, almost obsessive thoughts, were for Susan, but he knew that was a dream unlikely to be realized.

He decided to go to Scotland. He had to thank the old man for that favour. It would be a perfect place to recuperate from the excesses of the last few months and it would be nice to see Rowena again. He sent a wire to her and she delightedly told him to come up right away. He put his few affairs in order, stopped for a few days to see Father, Mother, and sister, none of whom had changed. Father was vaguely aware that he had been away, but not sure where; Mother was still disinterested and looking wan, and Molly was adoring and anxious.

"You look so tired my dear. Go to Scotland and rest."

He had told her about Rowena. She encouraged Cecil to follow his heart. So he left and made the journey back to the castle on the Loch.

When he debarked from the train and before he saw her, he heard her "Darling. It's so wonderful to see you again."

He'd forgotten how lovely she was, that tumbling thick beautiful auburn hair, that shapely face, straight delicate nose and marvellous mouth that had kissed him so excitingly and extravagantly so long ago, her large green eyes. It was cold, so she was wrapped in heavy woollen sweaters and scarves, but he could feel her warmth through all that, her body trembling, her heart beating.

Cecil had taken the little puffer from the harbour on the mainland that brought mail and provisions to the island every week. She had met him at the small dock. Now they were walking, arms around each other, suddenly it seemed as though all the fears and dangers of the past were being washed away, washed away by her loving laughing warmth. Events that had happened, both good and bad, now appeared distant and without meaning or importance. This combination of her presence and the magical surroundings of wind and sky and distant hills and calling sea birds enveloped him. He couldn't help himself, he cried with relief. She stopped and held him.

"Yes my dear cry. Get it all out."

"Oh I'm so sorry. It's just so marvellous to be here with you again. I can't tell you how lovely this is."

"No don't. It's all right. I love you my sweet and I will look after you."

He wiped his wet face. "I feel so silly."

"Well you're not silly. You've been through a bad time."

"Thank you my love."

They reached the house.

"Father's still away doing stuff about demobilisation, poor dear. He might make it this weekend though."

"Oh, good. I'm dying for a drink."

"And you shall have one my sweet."

He had several. They sat close together on the old leather couch. The Wolfhounds lay at their feet and snored. The fire crackled in the great stone hearth. Rowena snuggled in his arms. Dinner, he had been assured, was being prepared by the live-in cook and housekeeper, and was, by the delicate but robust fragrance wafting from the kitchen, going to be something quite special. Cecil thought "This is as good as it's ever going to get."

Rowena's father never did make it in time to see Cecil, but he and Rowena spent three incredible days and nights together, loving and laughing and falling in love. The time came though, when Cecil had to go back to England and find some sort of meaningful employment. They discussed his prospects together and agreed that it would be better for him to see what he could find in London. Then perhaps she could join him.

When they parted ,it was a grey, cold, and windy day. The clouds scudded low and fast across the loch. The little boat rocked. Cecil stepped gingerly onto the coaming and jumped down to the deck.

"Be careful my darling."

"Yes, I will, dear Rowena. I love you."

"I love you. Write soon."

"Will do."

The boat's engine burbled into life and they sheered off from the dock. The handful of locals gave a weak cheer and waved. The ferry put-putted away. Cecil looked back. Rowena's red hair was the last thing he saw. She was waving.

CASTING ABOUT...

Sitting one night in a pub in London, he had found near the temporary lodgings he had moved into, glancing through the jobs available, he realised that employment was going to be hard to find. He was like thousands of young ex-officers who had gone straight into action from school. None of them had any profession or trade to go into. They knew nothing. Soldiering was their only expertise. 'Lets see. Door-to-door salesman. Horrors! Can't face that. Factory work. No good. Experience needed.'

"Hello Paynter." He looked up. A tall, dark, mustached man stood there smiling.

"Hello. What are you doing here?" asked Cecil, without the faintest idea who this was.

"I live around the corner. Buy you a drink?"

"Thanks. Pint of bitter please." As the stranger moved to the bar Cecil racked his brains. I know I know him, but where and when?

"You don't remember me do you?" the man said, putting glasses down.

"No, I'm terribly sorry. I know we've met, but where?"

"I met you at that Chateau in France. You came in looking like a drowned rat. I showed you the bathroom."

"Of course, you're the rifleman. Right."

"Spot on. Name's Adair. John Adair.

"Of course. Good to see you again.

"So, looking for a job?"

"Yes. Not much luck I m afraid."

"No there's not much for us chaps. I might be able to find you something if you're interested though."

"You bet." I'll try anything, so long as its reasonably honest."

Well, it's certainly that. I'm a copper."

"Good God!" said Cecil. "Plain clothes?"

"Yes. We're looking for gentlemen who've had some experience commanding men. That's you. You would start on the beat after training, with the rank of Police Constable. Do that for a year or so, then into civvies and you go on special assignment. It will all be explained later. Lord Trenchard's re-organising the Metropolitan Police. Recruiting ex-army officers is his idea. What do you think?"

"Gosh, this is so unexpected I don't know what to say, but I'm interested."

"Capital! Here's my card. Come and see me in the morning. New Scotland Yard, ten o'clock. OK?"

"Right, I'll be there."

Cecil arrived dutifully on time and went across the courtyard to the back door where he saw a sign saying police and cadet entrance. He followed two burly men in raincoats and trilby hats, who held the glass swing doors open for him.

"Wotcher mate!" one said with a grin. Joining up?

"Looks like it," Cecil answered.

"You'll love it. You going to be an obbo officer?

"I don't know what that means said Cecil."

"You soon will."

The right office was found, and Cecil, being the only one there that day, was soon sitting at Detective Inspector Adair's desk (for that is what the little sign on the desk said).

The interview was long and thorough, and successful. Cecil walked out, on air. He had been accepted as probationary police cadet being entirely the sort of chap they were looking for, as Adair put it.

Later that week he received a bulky buff envelope with "On His Majesty's Service" printed on it. In it were instructions as to where to report, with rail warrant to the destination: the College at Hendon, north London.

He smiled, the warrant was for only a few pence, as Hendon was a short tube trip from where he was. The police were obviously very thorough with matters of petty cash.

He reported on the specified date and was soon whisked away into the life of a cadet for one of the great police forces of the world. Uniformed, medically examined, lectured, marched up and down, and generally made to feel that he was back in the army, except now he was a lowly private taking orders, not giving them. He lived with ten other recruits in a dormitory-like room that reminded him of school. His whole life seemed to be going backwards. Somehow though, he was happy and at ease.

The classes were interesting and not overly taxing. Some

of the others were mere boys and he was able to help them with their difficulties, so he soon became liked and respected. The days and weeks passed quickly and contentedly.

He wrote to his family and friends to tell them of his situation. The answers were interesting and telling, varying from utter horror from his Mother, puzzled surprise from his father, approval from brother and sister, and delight and encouragement from Rowena and her father, asking him to visit the castle on his first leave.

The period of transformation from 'wet behind the ears' to the passing-out parade, went by quickly and relatively painlessly. His father and sister came, his mother had practically disowned him so did not attend. His brother was busy somewhere. The occasion passed without untoward incidents. He was now a Bobby!

After a short leave, too short to go to Scotland, Cecil was assigned to his first posting.

DERELICT DE LUXE...

Cecil was to work out of Tottenham Court Road Police Station, C Division. A mixed blessing. This was a notoriously edgy part of town: the area forming the grimier part of the so-called West End, the theatre, cafe, and entertainment district. One moved carefully here. A look of blank disinterest was the expression best adopted.

Here, behind the ratty shops with fly-blown windows, deals were done involving the dubious contents of small brown suitcases and parcels filled with wrinkled paper. Money. Drugs. Information. Anything of value. This was a place of shadows. Business of the most sinister type was done here. Life at its most tawdry was lived in this hellhole. Turn left onto Goodge Street for a good time. Pass the clothing factory, on your left, cross the wet cobbles, don't turn down that road. There danger lies. Best avoided. Some very nasty people lived in a tangle of alleyways and *cul de sacs* here. No, go instead on to where melancholy and suffering wait to be attended to. It was that part of London that lurked at the edges, with sightless windows and unwelcoming doors. Such sad little shops that did exist, sold items that would interest only the lost, lonely, and the hopeless. Dirty books, apparatus for the limbless, the halt, and the lame. Promises of the most bizarre experiences. Dust and decay lay on everything. Glass filmed with grime, covered messages on post cards to the lonely. Flats and rooms to let were indicated with much elaboration and exaggeration as to the qualities of furnishings and situation. Offers were directed to those with hairy upper lips.

"Write in complete confidence to Frederica Von something-or-other. No harmful depilatories, no electric needles, etc., etc." Peeling cinema posters and torn advertisements for boxing matches hung forlorn.

Here then, was where he was to spend the next year or two, learning from the old hands, dealing with the day-to-day domestic disputes, reports of smash–and-grab raids, burglaries, directing traffic, comforting victims of violence and outrage, accident and loss. He was lucky, in that most of the incidents were of a minor nature, the odd mad dog report where the constable had to collect the mad dog kit, which consisted of a long pole with a running noose and a pair of enormous asbestos gauntlets reaching up to the elbows, and then proceed to the address given, usually in some wretched tenement up some forgotten alleyway ,often to be told to "piss off copper."

He lost his helmet one night when he bent down to pat a cat and it fell off down an area fenced and locked. He had to rouse an indignant sleepy tenant to ruefully ask for his helmet back please.

He was rather pleased with the time on point duty when he was addressed by a rather slick looking driver of a long, low car, who, calling him "Charley" asked the way to Madame Tussaud's Waxworks.

Cecil said "How did you know my name was Charley sir?"

"Well I suppose I guessed it," answered the slick one.

"Well you can bloody well guess your way to Madame Tussaud's sir." Then Cecil turned back to direct the traffic.

Cecil had found a small bed-sitter in one of those little streets just off Baker Street not far from the tube station. It was clean, with a bed, a table, a little fireplace, a big comfy arm chair, a side table, a large mahogany wardrobe, and in one corner, a washbasin and mirror. The fireplace had quite a handsome mantelpiece with another mirror over that. There was a large bogus Turkish carpet that almost covered the whole room. The floor was wood. There were some lights in wall sconces and a standing lamp that sat behind the chair. Altogether it was quite cozy with the curtains drawn and the fire on. There was, as well, a small bookcase, which Cecil soon loaded with all his collection.

Outside the room on the landing, was a small gas cooker and a tiny larder with fretted wire doors. The rules were strict: no lady friends; no noise after ten p.m. As Cecil worked long hours, he didn't mind this at all, only using the place to eat, sleep, and be alone in. Special arrangements were made with the landlady regarding the odd shift hours Cecil had to keep.

An important part of any young man's life in Great Britain, is to find a good pub nearby. This will be where his social life happens for much of his spare time. This is where he will find consoling friends, good chums, and understanding from all. Cecil found just the place, conveniently just around the corner. It was called The Welbeck and was on the street of the same name.

In short order he made friends with several amusing people, some married, some, like him, still single. He was quickly adopted and made much of, particularly by some older women who were either wives or friends of some of the others. Many of the men were ex-servicemen, mostly commissioned officers and mostly army. Lots of battles were fought over again those evenings by the coal fire in the saloon bar.

As was proper in those days gentlemen and ladies drank in the saloon bar or the private bar. The lads of the factories and offices drank with their women in the public bar. It was an unwritten rule then, and crossover intrusions were rare. Prices were less for the working man.

Hours were very strict. Drinking began at eleven a.m., went until three, then the place was closed and cleaned, to reopen at five, and then closed again for the night at eleven.

The day after his probationary period ended, he was introduced to the job he had been recruited for. This was to be an observation officer, known in the service as "obbo officer." It entailed being in civilian clothes and playing the part of an undergraduate, going to drinks clubs which proliferated throughout the west end, and making sure no one was served after hours. If and when this happened, he would report the illegal incident to headquarters, who would then, next evening, raid the place. Often the owner of the nightspot would plead innocence, whereupon, not realising that there had been a plain clothes officer observing, PC Cecil would be marched into court as witness for the prosecution. Not a very nice business. In fact, positively nasty, and probably illegal, but as London was going through a period of lawlessness, a necessary evil. He went through this period carrying out his duties o the letter but hating every minute of it,

It was on a job at a notorious after hours drinks club called The Black Cat that Cecil first met the Grey Brothers. Two nastier types it would be hard to find. They ran a clutch of bars, some small back-room gambling, and some prostitution rings which they controlled with a special brutality and viciousness.

Cecil was sitting at the bar nursing a small light ale and trying to look like an undergrad down for the day, when one of the brothers came up and said "You an obbo officer?"

"Excuse me?"

"You 'eard. You ain't got cloth ears."

"I don't know what you mean."

"Orl right. Come over 'ere. My bruvver and I want a word with yer."

"Oh very well." Cecil drained his glass, almost choking. He was very frightened.

The table the other brother was sitting at had another occupant. Cecil recognized him, his picture was always in the papers. Joe Robinson, another nasty piece of work, and, Cecil thought, an enemy of the Grey Brothers. They seemed friendly enough now though.

" 'Ave a pew copper' said Tommy Grey, the older brother and the boss.

"I think you have me mixed up with someone else," said Cecil.

"Naow. It's orlright. We know 'oo you are. Relax we're not going to 'urt you, though we should. You've caused us a bit of bovver since you came on the scene."

"Okay. It's a fair cop," said Cecil. They all laughed.

"Now," said Tommy " 'eres the picture. You look the other way now and again and you'll find a nice little package under the tree at Christmas."

Cecil thought, 'If I'm going to get out of here without having my throat cut, I'd better box clever for a bit.'

"Hmm. Well it does sound tempting. Can I think about it a bit?"

"Yes, of course. Take your time. Five minutes orlright?"

Cecil swallowed hard.

"Well, if you put it like that, what can I say?"

"That's right. Cecil, isn't it? We shall keep an eye on you and see 'ow it goes. We'll take a keen interest in your welfare and progress, if you know what we mean. You'll be like a son to us. Orl right now. Fuck off and don't come back."

Cecil made his way back to the station as quickly as he could and reported the whole incident to the Chief Inspector, who put his fingers together and looked into space.

"Well, you're not much use to us now your cover is blown. We shall have to consider what to do with you. For the time being report to Sergeant Jones. He'll give you a desk job for a while. Stay close to home. Alright, go away and try to stay out of trouble.

Trouble, however, came looking for Cecil, and it didn't waste any time. A week later he was going home and had decided to stop for a quick one at his local. He had ordered a pint of bitter and was just lighting a cigarette when he felt a tap on the shoulder. He looked round.

"Where 'ave you bin Cecil?"

"Oh, hello Fred." It was one of the brothers.

"We've missed you round the clubs. Where 'ave you bin? Not ill are you, not indisposed I trust. Give us a pint darling." The peroxided barmaid patted her hair and fluttered her eyelids.

"No, I'm fine. A bit busy at the office, you know."

"No, I don't know. I just 'ope you're keeping your end of the bargain up. It wouldn't do to cross us bruvvers now, would it?"

No, of course not. Well I must be off."

"Yes, of course. Off you go. I'm glad we 'ad this little chat. We shall be keeping an extra close eye on you and yours (he gave an unpleasant wink) if you know what I mean."

After this incident Cecil decided to talk to Gerald and seek his advice.

Later that evening he was sitting in the drawing room of the house in Belgravia drinking whiskey with Gerald. They chatted inconsequentially about the war. Cecil was trying to screw up the courage to confide in Gerald. Gerald was recounting some amusing stories about his last few weeks at the front.

"Yes we were resting near Poperinghe and some athletics

had been organised. The cups and medals were distributed by the silly old duffer commanding the division, who made a speech afterwards, saying rather unexpectedly 'Congratulations on running so well. I hope you run as well when you meet the enemy,' then ending his admonitions with the words: 'You are a fine battalion. My only regret is that I won't be with you when you fight the Hun.' Then someone in the back shouted, 'You can 'ave my fucking place anytime mate.' This brought a howl of laughter from the men and a wan smile from the general."

Later, after dinner, sipping brandy and smoking cigars, Gerald said, "Did you enjoy the staff job?"

"How did you know about that?" asked Cecil, in surprise. "I never mentioned it."

"Well who do you suppose got it for you?"

"Your father?"

"Yes."

"My God. I had no idea." I thought it was Rowena's father.

"No. Pater thought you were marvellous getting me to the palace that day. That was his way of saying thanks."

Cecil and Gerald spent the next few days together. Cecil had a few days off, so was able to relax while waiting for a good time to bring up his problems.

One morning he woke up to find that they were off to Bedfordshire to shoot pheasants on someone's estate. Though Cecil didn't relish standing about in some damp field waiting to kill some unfortunate bird, he still had not been able to bring himself to confide in Gerald about his troubles, so he went. He was a good shot and that evening at the old house, the family made him welcome, and other than almost breaking a tooth on some shot when chewing a wing, he had a really good time.

Finally one evening he got Gerald alone and confided to him his predicament with his job.

"Never thought you would like the police. Told Pater so."

"Well I quite like some aspects of it, I just don't enjoy the spying part."

"No, I can certainly understand that.

"I've also managed to spend more than I make and so have to continue to work to try to bring my debts down. I've also managed to get involved with some unpleasant characters who are getting threatening. He told him about the Grey Brothers.

He had tried other friends. They seemed to vanish when loans were mentioned. In desperation, and with more hope than anticipation, he tried his father. His father read him the riot act, culminating in a resounding NO!

Somehow Rowena had heard of his predicament. He received a letter offering to help. She said that she had not much cash but he was welcome to what she had. Though tempted, he felt uncomfortable about borrowing from her, and refused.

Though he was very much in love with Rowena he felt that there was more that he should do to clear up all the difficulties that surrounded him. He had to prove his worth as much to himself as to the world about him.

Thoughtlessly, stupidly, he mentioned in his letter a diffidence towards any further romantic attachments, giving as his reasons, false claims to obligations of an occupational nature. He vaguely referred to opportunities in the Middle East. He had, in fact, thought about joining his brother who had become an officer in the Egyptian Police Force and who was presently in Cairo. His brother could probably get him a job there. The problem was, how to get there, strapped as he was for the wherewithal.

Gerald said, "You are in trouble. Didn't realise it was quite that bad. Look, don't worry. I'll have a word with Father."

After breakfast on the morning he was to go back to work, the general asked him to come into his study for a chat.

"Gerald tells me you're short of cash, that right?"

I'm afraid so sir. I do have plans, but, er... ." he trailed away.

"Yes, yes, of course, of course. Well I am willing to make you a small advance on one condition. I believe that you should perhaps, leave England. I'm very fond of you and am grateful for how you helped me with my son, but now I think you should be separated for your own good. Acceptable?"

Cecil told him about his tentative thoughts about Egypt.

"Why that's capital, capital. A splendid idea! I have friends there who will help you." He turned to his desk and scribbled something on a piece of paper.

"How will this do? You can pay me back when you make your fortune, what, what?"

Cecil gazed at the cheque, for that's what it was. A cheque for five hundred pounds.

"Really sir, I don't know how to thank you."

"Not at all. Now go out there and make us all proud of you. Good luck my boy."

In the next post he received a letter from Rowena with an edge of coldness in its contents. She quite understood how he felt. Good luck in his future endeavours. etc., etc. Hoped they would always be friends, and so on.

TO EGYPT...

Cecil arranged an appointment to see his divisional commander and asked for his permission to resign. The fact that he was going to the police force in Egypt made the severance problem less difficult. In fact, he was congratulated on his initiative and wished good luck.

He spent the next few days writing to his friends and family with news of his plans. He sent a telegram to Nigel in Egypt with details of the travel arrangements he had made with Messrs Thomas Cooke & Co., and last, but not least, he made arrangements through an acquaintance to disburse funds to cover his gambling debts.

Having got his passport, received the necessary injections and inoculations for travel to Egypt and beyond, he packed his bags and made his farewells, Cecil wearily climbed the gangway to board the SS Baraboole, a P & O Liner, at Tilbury. The Baraboole was a veteran of the England to Australia shipping route which went via Port Said at the northern end of the Suez Canal, on to Bombay in India, and then to Sydney. She lay there in the midday glare, dull black funnel, yellow ochre superstructure, deep black hull. Derricks and cranes were hoisting bales and crates. Stevedores were running up and down service gangways. The smells of the sea and ships, steam, oil, tarred rope, coal, and fresh paint were redolent everywhere.

"Good morning sir. Welcome aboard." An officer took his papers and travel documents.

"Ah, Port Said. Right sir. Steward, show Mr. Paynter his cabin."

Cecil followed the steward, threading his way through the crowds of fellow passengers and visitors.

A band was playing light music somewhere. There was an air of excitement and pleasurable anticipation. Cecil started to feel better. 'A quick brandy and soda will fix me up,' he thought.

" 'Ere we are sir. Your cabin. You'll be sharing with another gentleman. You'll be quite comfortable I'm sure. 'Eres the bathroom. All the comforts of home I'm sure. Why thank you sir, thank you." He pocketed the modest tip and slipped out through the door.

After paying off all his debts, he had only enough for second class, which, in those days, wasn't all that bad. The cabin was small and sparse, but the bunks looked alright. He looked out of the porthole. They were just above the waterline. Cecil threw some tepid water in his face, washed his hands and brushed his hair. At that moment there was a knock at the door.

"Yes?"

"We're casting off in a few minutes sir, just in case you want to be up top."

"Oh thanks steward."

As he climbed the companion-way to the upper deck, Cecil could feel and hear the throbbing and the deep resonance of the engines starting up deep down in the bowels of the ship, and as he came out into the sunshine, the sounds were almost lost in the noise of bands and cheering as the ship's crew prepared to cast off lines.

The visitors had all gone ashore and the ship seemed to be straining to leave. Cecil looked up at the foremast and saw, fluttering at the head, the Blue Peter, the ensign that tells the world 'I am about to sail.' The band broke into Auld Lang Syne and hankies came out for the last tears.

The ship began to move, first forwards, then backwards, as the tugs took hold and exerted their weight, and thrust. Then a pause. Then the whole giant craft trembled and surged forward, smoke billowing from her funnel. The sound of the band faded. The cheering became indistinct. Having broken all contact with the land, the SS Baraboole sailed down the River Thames, heading for the open sea.

Cecil sat in a deckchair looking about him. There were a few passengers lining the rail as the ship passed down the river, otherwise he was alone As he watched the emerald fields of Kent slip by, an enormous feeling of melancholy fell over him. He felt waves of sadness, and more, he felt apprehensive. What on earth was he doing leaving the land he loved so much and the woman that he had rediscovered such deep feelings for? Surely he could have found some other method of paying off his debts. The Grey Brothers could have been squared somehow. But he did have this over-riding desire to make something of himself before going to Rowena as a suitable suitor. Pull your socks up Paynter. Look ahead. Everything will turn out all right. Hmmm, a brandy and soda will cheer me up.

Cecil found his way to the second class lounge and cocktail bar. It was crowded. A convivial, noisy, smoke-filled room, stewards scurrying about. He threaded his way to the bar and found an empty stool.

"Brandy and soda please, bartender."

"Yes sir. Ice?"

"Please."

The drink arrived. He sipped. 'Perfect.'

He lit a cigarette.

"Ahh!"

He looked around, then turned to his neighbour, a young man dressed in a uniform Cecil did not recognise.

"Hello," he said.

"Oh, hello," answered the stranger. "Where are you off to?"

"I'm going out to join my brother in Cairo."

"Oh really? What does he do?"

Cecil told him and of his plans to join the police.

"Well good luck old boy its getting a bit dicey out there. King Fuad doesn't like us too well and he's stirring things up a bit."

"What are you?" asked Cecil.

"I'm a *Bimbashi* in the Sudan Police. Khartoum actually."

"Oh, interesting."

"Yes, you might try us. It's a great life down there. The

Sudanis are much better than the Gyppos. Lots of hunting and fishing. What are you drinking?"

After dinner, quite exhausted, Cecil decided on one gentle walk around the deck and to bed. It was getting dark, but he could still see the land on either side as the ship cleared the Thames estuary. Ahead, the English Channel gleaming like molten copper in the setting sun waited to dismay those passengers prone to seasickness.

A persistent creaking noise woke Cecil up. The ship was rolling heavily. He looked at his watch. The middle of the night. He sat up and looked over at his cabin mate whom he had met briefly just before the lights were doused. and who had turned out to be a rather strait-laced and reserved missionary going to India, and who was probably praying that he could get there quickly, for the sounds emanating from his bunk spoke of the miseries of mal du mer.

The next morning the sea had calmed down a little, although not enough for the missionary, who stayed groaning and green in his bunk the whole day. Cecil fortunately was alright other than a slight headache. The rolling main wasn't affecting him. He ate a hearty breakfast of Scotch Kippers, brown toast and hot strong tea, after which he went for a walk around the deck and then wrote letters until lunch. This shipboard routine continued as day followed day: breakfast, a walk, a deck chair with blanket, and hot boullion at eleven. Then a pink gin ,followed by lunch, a nap, a walk, tea at four, drinks at six, dinner at seven, and after that to the saloon to play bridge until bed at midnight. The weather was reasonable until they hit the Bay of Biscay, which, keeping to its evil reputation, was stormy with the seas high and steep. Then the left turn past Gibraltar and into the calm, aquamarine Mediterranean. Blissful days and nights, warm and smooth seas, the stars at night sparkling and mysterious in the deep vault of purple velvet.

Valetta was reached, and those few disembarking for the island of Malta took their leave. The next few days passed quickly. Cecil played deck hockey, quoits, and swam in the small pool on the promenade deck. Altogether life was rather perfect. He wondered how hard it would be to go back to work. In fact though, he was eager to get to whatever job Nigel was going to get for him. Fun and games can't go on for ever.

Early on the day they were to arrive at Port Said, Cecil got up at six and walked to the foremost part of ship that was accessible to passengers. He had his binoculars with him. He set his elbows firmly on the rail and put the glasses to his eyes. He twiddled the knurled rings until the horizon sharpened and clarity was achieved. He then turned his body to face south and looked carefully. 'Yes, there it was,' that unlikely streak of what looks like blurred cloud but is in fact a land mass. A peculiar thrill is always felt by even the most jaded traveller at sea when this moment arrives. The distant formless picture begins to transform into more familiar shapes, in this case the yellow ochre and white sands of the North Egyptian shore. The closer they got to land one could begin see houses and mosques, then as they passed Alexandria, they were close enough to see bathers in the surf and small craft with people waving and calling. It was just dusk as the boat tied up to a buoy in the harbour of Port Said.

Immediately they were swarmed by small boats packed with Arabs offering every conceivable service and item from bananas to someone's readily available sister. Other more official craft elbowed these illegal but persistent hawkers to one side with much waving of arms and vociferous language. These were the customs and police. Cecil was all ready with his papers to disembark, and the process of moving from ship to shore was accomplished with a minimum of fuss.

"Hello old boy. Good trip?" It was his brother.

"Capital. Thanks Nigel. Good to see you."

"I expect you could use a drink. There's a nice little bar in the hotel."

"Gharry," he called to a horse-drawn carriage.

"In you get Cecil."

The whole equipage moved out into the traffic of the street. Clip-clopping, the grinning Arab driver yelled obscenities at all around. The horse whinnied and farted and tossed its head, accoutrements jingling. Cecil looked around at the scene in wonder. There in the distance was the column of the Ferdinand De Lesseps statue, the builder of the great canal that the Baraboole would be sailing down on the way to the Red Sea and India tomorrow. He looked back and had one last look at the old ship as she lay there lit by arc lights, resting after her voyage, resting and being attended to by scores of stevedores and coalers feeding her for her continuing journey to the east.

The noise of the crowds of people moving about them, along with the clopping hooves, the creak and clatter of wood and iron and leather and the jingle of the brass bells, prevented any attempt at conversation without shouting, so they gave up trying and just looked around at the colourful animated scene, and occasionally looked at each other and grinned.

They arrived at a small but clean hotel that catered to travellers en route to Cairo. They booked in and had a drink and chatted about home and the prospects for Cecil. Before long though, Cecil's drink and the exhaustion from his travels began to make their effects felt. A great lassitude come over him as he contemplated his unknown future in this very foreign place so distant from home. He asked to be excused and retired to bed early.

It was dark when Cecil awoke, around midnight from the sleep-blurred hands of his watch. He was alarmed by the sound of drums penetrating his exhaustion, beating a repetitive tattoo. He went to find Nigel, who reassured him with a laugh: they were only wedding drums celebrating someone's nuptials, a sound he would hear most nights henceforth in the Middle East.

Early the next morning they boarded the train to Cairo, and upon arrival, they got another gharry to negotiate the distance and take them to the Shepheard Hotel, the grand old lady of the Middle East. Eventually the gharry pulled out of the traffic and swept up the drive to the front door.

"My God," said Cecil. "I can't afford this place."

"Oh we'll just be here for a couple of nights. It's on me. I can't afford more than that myself. And we need a night on the town."

"Splendid," said Cecil.

Turbaned *Suffragis* in white with green cummerbunds and grinning white teeth ran down the steps and grabbed the bags, while Nigel paid the gharry driver. Cecil slowly mounted the steps looking up at the great imposing front of the famous hotel. Elegantly dressed women tripped past him rippling with laughter like a flight of exotic birds, their scents overlaying the perfume of mimosa and frangipani that came from the bushes and trees that grew abundantly in the hotel grounds.

'I'm going to like this,' thought Cecil.

Nigel caught up with him as the commissionaire opened the glass swing door.

"What do you think?"

"Fantastic. Where's the bar?"

"Let's book in first," said Nigel with a smile.

They crossed the hall. The floors were marble, waxed, shining. Great glittering mirrors framed in gold hung along the walls, reflecting and enlarging the rooms and halls. There were palms in massive brass containers everywhere. Fans revolved far above, cooling the air that felt pleasant and dry after the heat and humidity of the Cairenne day outside.

They threaded their way through the quite crowded vestibule and reached the great dark mahogany check-in counter.

"Would you please register sir?" The tall immaculate Egyptian proffered pen and paper.

"Ah yes, thank you." Nigel registered too and handed the completed forms back to the clerk.

"Oh yes, the Mr. Paynters. Room 21. Boy! Take the gentlemen to their rooms. Have a pleasant stay sirs."

"This looks jolly nice," remarked Nigel as they were shown into their rooms. It was large, with high ceilings and French windows that were open to a small balcony. The inevitable and essential fan was turning slowly above them.

"I could use a cold bath," said Cecil.

"Right old boy, you go on. I'll order drinks. Gin slings alright?"

"Right on," said Cecil.

The bath was delicious, the gin slings, even better. They had both dressed for dinner, Cecil in dinner jacket, Nigel in the mess dress of the Egyptian Police. He looked especially elegant and was eyed hungrily by the ladies, and, Cecil noticed, by some of the men. They made their way down the staircase to the dining room. Dinner was prolonged and impressive: cold soup, turbot, small delicate quails, a spectacular dessert which consisted of ice cream, mangoes, whipped cream and meringue, the whole smothered in chocolate and triple sec. Turkish coffee and cigarettes completed this Ali Babean feast.

"Let's do the town now. Come on Cecil."

"Oh I'm exhausted dear boy."

"Nonsense. We're going night clubbing."

"Ooh, alright," groaned Cecil. "Tired, yes. Dead, no."

"Off we go."

After a tumultuous hackney ride through the warm palm-

When The Devil Drives

lined streets, they came to the famous *Auberge des Pyramides*, the fabled night club situated near the Pyramids of Giza. The configuration of this den of iniquity is of a gigantic Bedouin tent. It is lavishly furnished with Turkish and Persian carpets of immense proportions and luxuriousness, together with furniture of such abandoned tastelessness that the most excessive lover of egregious and over-the-top sophistry would cry "enough!"

With much bowing, saluting, and scraping, entry was obtained. The place was packed. The dress on both sexes was ornate and colourful and matched the furniture in a frenzy of cloth. Feathers, ribbons, silk, jewellery, all was inspired madness. The music of an Arab orchestra wailed and drummed in the main restaurant. A belly dancer, a pale Circassian with skin like satin, glided and undulated among the tables. The floor, of black mirror-like tile, shone and glittered like cold ice reflecting her moves. Great fans high above circulated the air. The atmosphere was, Cecil thought, utterly gorgeous in an outrageously decadent way.

The *maitre d'* showed them to a table at the edge of the dance floor. It was covered in a snow-white damask cloth on which were the usual napkins and cutlery.

"We're not eating," said Nigel airily. "You can take all this away and bring us a bottle of *Veuve*."

"Yes sir. Of course sir."

The offending implements were whisked away and a frosty silver bucket placed at their table. At a signal from the sommelier, who was attending, a waiter appeared with a bottle of champagne, uncorked it with a soft plop, and deftly wrapping it in a napkin, poured the golden bubbly into the glasses.

"Ah, this is the life," said Nigel, taking a long drink. "Cigarette?"

In no time Nigel had picked up two French girls at the next table and frivolous and bibulous times followed. Cecil found himself whirling around the floor with first one girl and then with the other. The next few hours would be a blur in Cecil's memory. He remembered vaguely being helped into a taxi with one of the girls, whose name was Mimi, and who was, if anything drunker than he was, and he remembered being driven through the streets of the city to the hotel. After that, blankness, until waking with a crashing hangover sprawled across the bed, sans clothes, and, he was relieved to note, alone.

More blessed sleep followed. No one bothered him so that it was late afternoon before he woke and staggered to the bathroom. It had not impinged on his mind that Nigel was nowhere to be seen, so it was with surprise, that as he was brushing his teeth, he heard his brother's voice bidding him a good afternoon.

"Where the hell have you been?"

"Oh, don't ask old boy. That French girl had me in knots. I'm worn out. I'm going to bed. We have to be up at the crack of dawn tomorrow. I have an appointment for you with Ferguson at nine and I've got to be there with you. I've arranged a call for seven."

Cecil dressed and went to the telephone and ordered room service for two for dinner. It was then about six. He went to where the drinks were, on a small table, and poured himself a stiff brandy and soda. Then, lighting a cigarette, he went out onto the balcony and sat on a wicker chair. He drank a little of the drink and drew on the cigarette. He surveyed the scene.

The Nile glittered in the evening sunset, a couple of lateen-sailed feluccas floated past. Some laughter from the garden below. A muezzin called the faithful to prayer.

'God!' he thought, 'the other week I was in a taxi in London in the rain.'

Dinner came. It was an omelet. They ate quietly. Bed came early.

Recruitment And Training...

Smartly at eight fifty-five on the dot, Cecil and Nigel presented themselves to the office of *Bimbashi* Ferguson. Cecil had discovered that *"Bimbashi"* was Turkish for "Major." They were shown into a light, bright, room, completely bare except for a large desk and a couple of chairs. At the desk sat an angry-looking, red-faced officer.

He looked up from some papers he was studying and snorted, "What do you two warts want? I hope you don't smoke. Filthy habit! Just gave it up myself."

Cecil noticed an ashtray on the desk. There were some butts and ash in it.

"Well, not much sir."

"Drink?"

Nigel, quick as always blurted, "No, but we will if you want us to sir."

"What are you drivelling about? Well what do you want? I'm a busy man."

"This is my brother, sir. I told you about him. He's hoping you can take him as a temporary officer."

"Well. This is most irregular, and, I might add, bloody inconvenient. You warts think you can run roughshod over us all out here. But you're in luck Paynter. We had to send

Qabudan Foster home last week. Went potty. No stamina in you young chaps these days. I was just about to signal for a replacement."

'Terrific,' thought Cecil.

"Yes. Let's see... ." Ferguson shuffled through some papers. "Yes here we are. Were you in the last lot?"

"Yes sir. Scots Fusiliers. The Somme and third Ypres."

"Get anything up here?" Ferguson motioned to his left breast.

"Just Squeak and Wilfred sir." These were the slang names for the two war medals that everyone got.

"Oh. That's disappointing."

Cecil glanced at Ferguson's left breast and noticed a DSO and an MC along with all the others.

"School?"

"Downside, sir."

"Oh. Bloody mackerel snapper are we?"

Cecil swallowed his distaste and remained silent.

"Got a private income?"

"Afraid not sir."

"You don't have much, do you? Well beggars can't be choosers I suppose. Take him out and get him properly dressed. You know the drill. Tell Tucker to take him under his wing and show him his duties. Report back to me in a month and we shall see what we can do with Mr. Paynter.

"What the hell is a *"Qabudan"* Nigel?" asked Cecil afterwards.

"A Captain. You've gone up a step without doing

anything. But you are only temporary. You'll have to behave for a while. They will give you an exam before you even start the official probationary period.

The next few weeks passed quickly. A thorough and rather brutal medical examination; shots for all the diseases of the East, etc. etc.

"No drinking for twenty-four hours," said the doctor with a grin.

A visit to the clothes store for fundamentals, which included the distinctive headgear of the force, the so-called *Tarboosh* or *Fez* made of red felt with a jaunty black tassel hanging from the top and dangling down at the back; then on to the official tailor for the required uniforms: one for day, one for night; issue of personal weaponry, in this case the same revolver Cecil had in France, a trusty and reliable Webley .38, handy and reasonably accurate at short distances; and finally a rather smart black Sam Brown belt and black cap with the insignia of the force in front completed the outfit. Cecil thought he looked quite smart.

Cecil studied the rules and regulations of the force and practiced at the shooting gallery, as well as accompanying the officer to whom he had been assigned for training. This was a Peter Foster, who was quite a card. Apparently he had left England under a bit of a cloud, having blotted his copy book on numerous occasions while a soldier in France, and after demobilisation, in England, where he had joined the police as a constable. Chief amongst his misdemeanours, and the one that got him kicked out of the Metropolitan Police and then out of England, was when he borrowed the then-chief constable's Hillman squad car to take a debutante to the Queen Charlotte Ball at Grosvenor House, got drunk and wrecked the car on the Great North Road when taking the girl home.

Cecil's first assignment with *Qabudan* Foster was to go into the Arab quarter where the *souk,* or market, was. This was close to the great Citadel of Cairo, an ancient and venerable part of the city, but not the safest area for an infidel. They drove in a police car as far as they could and then had to go on foot. There were four of them: Peter, Cecil, and two Arab constables, all armed with revolvers.

They were met by a guide who was to take them to the scene of the crime: a domestic dispute over the ownership of some goats and chickens, which had led to the murder of one of the participant's several wives.

After a long and difficult negotiation, they were led through a complex of covered alleyways and arrived at the scene. The two constables, who were old hands, quickly cleared the onlookers away using their canes briskly against bare brown legs. The guide indicated the miscreants, who were standing there, shoulders drooping, eyes down, sheepish and shabby. A body lay covered with a khaki army blanket.

"Right," said Peter with authority. "Who's who and what's what here?"

A babble of Arabic explanations followed.

"Alright, alright," said Peter. "One at a time." Someone brought a chair out for him to sit on and then began a mini, but thorough and expert examination of all the players in this little tragedy.

Cecil watched, fascinated by this example of British justice and mores in this far-off exotic corner of the world. Here they were, two ordinary middle class Englishmen trying to do what they considered to be the right thing, their every word and gesture followed by the simple *Fellahin* who knew that whatever the outcome, these Ingleezi would do what was just and fair. The fact that these two pink foreigners were alone amongst hundreds of local folk who could have easily despatched them to Paradise, never entered the picture. This was how the Empire was run then, a mixture of public school confidence with a bit of bluff thrown in.

After a lengthy and arduous period of cross examination and close questioning, Peter closed his notebook and ordered the two policemen to manacle the suspect, and, clapping his hands together, said:

"Right. Back to the station. Off we go."

The whole party moved off, the officers leading the small parade, the rear party carrying the unfortunate victim's body on a makeshift stretcher.

At the station the duller side of police work was attended to: the filling out of forms, the name-taking, the details, that Abdullah Mohamed Bukta did on the 13th of December carry out an unlawful act of... , etc. etc. All important matters that Cecil had to know how to do; all the procedures that had to be followed; all the myriad details of police work.

Then there was the business of traffic and crowd control. There was the Nile and its busy traffic to supervise, illegal drug activity, robbery, extortion, prostitution, though much of the latter was so prevalent and so popular as to be virtually uncontrollable.

When the period of trial was over, Cecil was called to the office of his commanding officer who was surprisingly amiable and complimentary.

"Yes. Paynter." He cleared his throat a couple of times, snorted, and looked up from the papers he had been shuffling. "Yes, quite satisfactory. Must say, I am pleasantly surprised. You will have to sit for a formal exam, but I don't think you'll have any trouble there. Foster speaks highly of your behaviour and how quickly you have grasped the fundamentals of colloquial Arabic. Yes, splendid, splendid. You can put your pips up (the insignia of rank worn on both shoulders). Right. Well. Carry on. Foster will arrange matters concerning the written exam. Well done. You can go now."

As was right and proper, Cecil was taken out that night for an evening of celebration, a slap-up dinner at a good restaurant and a nightclub tour of formidable proportions.

TIME MARCHES ON...

The country of Egypt was, at this time (the mid 1920s) officially, a totally independent country with a constitution and a king whose name was Fuad. He ruled with the somewhat reluctant complicity of a Parliament. The truth was that Great Britain made all the rules, and, through a formally acknowledged treaty, saw that they were carried out. The person who saw to this was Sir Lee Stack, Great Britain's Governor General, or Viceroy, in the country. This arrangement had worked since the Ottoman Empire had relinquished its grip on the region in the 1880s.

Britain's influence had spread south into the Sudan, and, since the end of the war, into the north and east, Palestine, Trans Jordan, and Iraq – all countries put together by Britain after Turkey's surrender in 1918. To all intents and purposes *Brittannias Pax* seemed to work well, as it did in the Sudan, which, it was said, was a country of blacks ruled by blues, Britain having sent the cream of its best universities there to serve.

Cecil now was, in effect, at the sharp end of the stick again. As all the British Army Officers were dispensed with at the end of the war, many of them scattered to the outposts of Empire to become farmers, policemen, engineers, and soldiers for England and for others, some with success, some not. One or two places to which they all dispensed were not, strictly speaking, parts of the Empire, like Ireland and Palestine, both being examples oddly similar, inasmuch as the British were inserted between two warring factions, the one with furtive encounters in the mists and bogs and hatreds of hundreds of years, the other in the sands and deserts of the blood soaked Holy Land.

Cecil spent the days contented and happy in his work. He had to learn an enormous amount of detail about the administration of law in the country. He would have a probationary period of one year, attending classes where he would be expected to make an extensive study of criminal law and police procedure using a long list of books with titles like Egyptian Penal Code, The Criminal Procedure Code, The Evidence Act, The Manual of Medical Jurisprudence, The Egyptian Manual of First Aid, and The Police Drill Manual. It was a tedious and complex business, but it had to be attended to.

He got on well with the Arabs both in the city and in the country. He was liked by his constables and NCOs and was popular in the mess with his peers. His language skills were keen and he enjoyed learning the many and varied different tongues spoken here, then practising them when visiting outlying tribes, who in return gave him their respect as well as their usual lavish hospitality because of it. He was also getting to know and like all the other citizens of this exotic city: Jew, Syrian, Greek: mostly friendly and well-meaning, and all dealing with each other with relative amiability and good sense. The hotheads of the future were still to come.

The time passed quickly as it does when one is busy and happy. He sat for and passed his exams for the probationary period. The subjects Cecil had to master he found fascinating. The days went by in the classrooms of the Secretariat. A Maronite Egyptian came to his rooms twice a week to teach colloquial Arabic, which he found no trouble in learning.

The weeks and months passed. A year went by. The next few years were full of incident, some unpleasant, some routine, some exciting, like when the British Agent was murdered.

The telephone ringing by his bed woke him from a deep sleep.

"Yes. Paynter here. What? What's that? Yes. Yes, I'll be there at once." He hung up and sat on the edge of the bed trying to absorb the news. The Viceroy had been shot. He was, apparently, mortally wounded. Martial law had been declared. Cecil was to report to Police HQ for further orders.

It has always seemed, in recent times, that if the British people feel unfairly put upon by government or whatever, that they will go and protest somewhere, usually in good order, and often in a mild humour. In many cases it rains, and they finish up in a pub to grumble. There is rarely, if ever, violence of any kind. Such was not the case in unhappy Egypt, The poor *fellahin* held under the yoke, first of the corrupt and often cruel minions of the Ottoman rulers, then worked to death by the rich landowner, both Egyptian and foreign had reached the end of their tether. With the arrival of the British much of their misery had been alleviated. Just law was instituted and maintained without the brutalities of the past. In the case of the assassination of Sir Lee Stack, real and imagined slights and tribulations had been laid at the door of British governance, rightly or wrongly. But student unrest and violent street riots were occurring more frequently. Inevitably, the tenor of relationships between ruler and ruled was changing. Sometimes, not for the better.

Cecil reported at his office as requested, to find all the officers and men being organised for the expected trouble. He found himself being selected for the protection of the area around the centre of the city. In flat-out time he arranged his platoon of constables, choosing an enormous, very black Sudani corporal for his second in command. He fell them in outside, then quietly led them at the double, rifles at the trail, down the street towards the hub of the sleeping, but tense city.

Once in position, Cecil made his dispositions: a couple of men on a low roof overlooking the area, a couple at one end of a strategic cross-street, and then a single constable evenly placed in a line where a debouchment might be expected. He took up a central post with his corporal in the doorway of a shop. He had given orders to fire high in case there was trouble but to use the truncheon first. He checked his revolver, slipped off the safety, slid it back into his holster and fastened the clip. Now all they could do was wait.

Checking his watch, Cecil saw that it was 5:30. He listened for the *muezzin's* call to prayer. Just as the first weak glow in the eastern sky appeared, the wailing began, first from the one nearest them, then the others took up the call, until all the minarets of Cairo had joined in. People began to come out of their houses. Shops opened. Shutters were removed. The streets started to throng. Cecil breathed a sigh of relief. It looked like a false alarm. He and his men got a few curious looks, otherwise all was normal. He collected his group together and commenced the return to barracks.

When middle eastern tempers run high, a street mob is a very frightening thing. Though Cecil had not yet experienced one, he had heard stories from some of the old hands, so as nothing seemed to be happening he was feeling pleasantly relieved and relaxed, when the first signs of trouble began. First a distant sound of shouting. Then the noise of shattering glass and breaking wood. A smell came next. The smell of burning. Then smoke. Suddenly great rolling clouds of grey brown oily smoke.

Trying desperately to calm himself, he croaked out orders. "Right. Spread out." To the giant Sudanese, Abdullah: "Go to the left flank Ali." To one of the senior Arab constables: "Take two men and cover our rear." "Right. Load ball cartridge. Hold fire until I give the order, then fire over their heads."

Then, there they were, coming on at a run. The horde maddened and bent on destruction. A patter of stones fell on and around them. With just the soft headgear of the police uniform they had no protection against the rain of stones. And it got heavier. Cecil saw out of the corner of his eye, one of his men fall to his knees. His rifle dropped at his feet.

"Alright," Cecil addressed his thin khaki line, "prepare to fire high, over their heads. Present. Fire!"

The old Lee Enfields crashed out. The crowds paused. But then, seeing no one hurt. they came on shrieking. Sticks, stones, bricks, all the detritus of the streets came falling down on their heads. Cecil felt a sharp stinging pain on his forehead. 'Damn!' He drew his revolver.

"To hell with this. Right. Three rounds rapid. Aim at the legs. Fire!"

This time several bodies fell to the ground and the crowd stopped.

"Another round. Over the heads. Fire!"

This did the trick. The mob wavered and fell back.

"Right. Fix bayonets." Cecil gave the order he had last heard in France in 1918. "Steady. Advance."

At that moment, behind him Ali shouted.

"Effendi. Ingleeze soldiers coming." Cecil looked back.

'God what a relief.' Help was on the way. A company of British troops doubling up from behind,

"Need some help?" A young, tousled subaltern of Fusiliers ran past, grinning. The mob melted away as quickly as it had come.

Cecil sat on a box and mopped his brow. Only then did he realise that he was bleeding. 'My God, that was nasty,' he thought, as the soldiers, rifles at the port, hobnailed boots clattering, trotted past.

Back at headquarters Cecil was surrounded by fellow officers who had heard of his skirmish.

"Well done old boy."

"Good show old chap."

"Splendid effort," and so on. It was like being back at school when one had jumped higher or longer or ran faster than the others. It was exhilarating. Someone found a bottle of wine. Drinks all round.

"Tenshun!" Heels clicked. Glasses were dropped. The officer commanding had entered the room.

"As you were gentlemen. Stand easy."

Bimbashi Ferguson walked up to Cecil and looked him straight in the eye.

"Well done my boy. I hear you did good work today."

"Thank you sir. The men were splendid."

"Yes, well, good, good. I may have a job for you soon. come and see me in the morning. Right. Carry on gentlemen."

It transpired that the assassins were never caught, but the incident had brought to the surface some imponderables that were dealt with by Anglo-Egyptian relations being returned to their usual state of watchful and reluctant co-operation.

More months and years passed...

SPECIAL ASSIGNMENT...

Cecil was relatively happy. He had a group of friends with whom he worked and played. They, like most of their kind, enjoyed sports and the Anglo-Egyptian powers that be made sure there were ample facilities for them all. If for no other reason than to get their healthy young minds off the subject that allured them the most.

The only women out there in those days were the wives of senior officials. Mostly respectable. Those that weren't didn't last long. Nor did their lovers. Either they expired at the hands of angry husbands, or, more often, were sent home in disgrace. Sexual activities with indigenous ladies were frowned upon and were, in any case, risky, infectious diseases being rife and unpleasantly difficult to cure. So it was to be: cricket, tennis, sailing on the Nile, swimming in the Nile, playing squash at the Gezira Club, and now and again a round of golf at the one and only link in the country. Difficult and expensive to get into. All these activities did, however, lead to the same thing: drinks at the bar.

It would be gin slings, (gin and lemon juice with a maraschino cherry), gin and it, (this became the Martini later), pink gins (a mix of Angostura Bitters, crushed ice, and lots and lots of gin). Brandy and soda was popular with the older set, as was whisky and *moya* (or scotch and water, no ice of course), gin and tonic naturally, and gallons and gallons of cool beer, the glasses beading with moisture. Peanuts and skinny little cheese straws and olives and pimentoes, and tiny chipolata sausages were consumed by the bucketful.

After the drinks time, one went back to one's rooms and slept for an hour or so. Then one showered and dressed for dinner, in almost all cases, attended to by a servant, often a black Nubian from the Southern Sudan. Clothes were pressed and laid out on the bed, shoes shined, errands run. All in all, life was pretty good for the young colonial officer in Egypt in the late twenties and early thirties.

There was however, the odd spot of bother to cope with. It might be a minor disturbance in the city. Sometimes, clashes between British Tommies stationed on the canal and on leave in town and who thought rightly or wrongly that they had been gyped, the epithet created at the same time, as was "gyppo" or "gyppy tummy," like "Delhi Belly" on a different continent. All indicated something or someone unpleasant and tricky.

Sometimes there were larger and more dangerous disturbances; sometimes troubles to deal with in the deserts surrounding Cairo: one tribe against another over some goats or camels or women or melons. Whatever the reason there were always irritations that had to be allayed and dealt with fairly. Decisions of a Solomonic nature were made by men under the age of twenty five.

Cecil reported one day to *Bimbashi* Ferguson's office. He was kept waiting a few minutes. During that time another man arrived, a tall, spare, burnt-looking European. As he passed Cecil, he glanced at him, just a fleeting, casual look, but Cecil would never forget it. The eyes were blue ice and said "I am looking you over very carefully and making an immediate judgment as to your capabilities, your weaknesses, and general usefulness. I am then dismissing you."

The man strode on as if he owned the world, and went through the door without knocking. A few minutes later Cecil was summoned into that office. The stranger was lounging on the beat-up old leather divan drinking Turkish coffee, and from the smell of them, smoking the oval cigarettes from the same nation, pungent and fragrant.

"Coffee Paynter?"

"Thank you sir."

"*Suffragi!*" Ferguson yelled to the turbaned servant waiting at the door. "*Gib wahid Gahwa.* Cigarette?" the other man asked holding out an engine-turned cigarette case.

Cecil noticed that it bore an impressive looking armorial crest of some sort.

"Thomson, this is that promising young man I told you about. Paynter, this is Colonel Thompson. No doubt you have heard of him."

Of course Cecil had. This was the soldier who had explored much of the Sahara and most of the desolate areas west and south of Egypt. He had mapped the area right up to the border with the Italian Libyans, work that was to prove of critical value in the war that was going to come, they all knew, sometime in the future. During that war Thompson was to help organise and command a unit that became known as the Long Range Desert Group, an effective and highly regarded fighting command, respected by foe as well as by friend.

"Thank you sir." Cecil took the cigarette. Thompson lit it. Cecil took a long pull.

"Thanks."

"Now here's the form Paynter. Would you care to join a little excursion I'm planning, into The Great Sand Sea? I understand you speak the local lingo there?"

"Yes sir."

"Good. And I am told that you seem resourceful and are fairly quick on the uptake."

"I think so sir," said Cecil modestly.

"Well, fine. We leave next Thursday. Will you be with us?"

"Of course, sir. I would be honoured."

"Good. We meet at the Mena House Hotel on the road to Alex. Know it?"

"Of course sir."

"Right. Crack of dawn Thursday then. Goodbye."

Cecil floated out of the building. 'This was Heaven!' What every young man wanted to be in those days, was another Lawrence of Arabia. This was to be his chance. He hastened back to the mess and his rooms, to write letters and tell his chums of his good fortune.

"You jammy bastard," said one of the other officers. "We've been out here five years. You're here five bloody minutes and you get to go out and play in the desert with

Thompson. Crikey! Talk about luck."

They all crowded around congratulating, laughing, slapping him on the back.

"Well done."

"Good show."

"Lucky chap."

"Drinks all round."

Thursday came, Cecil had gone to bed early the night before so was up and drinking a scalding cup of coffee while he dressed. He had been told to dress comfortably and to prepare for cold nights, so he had chosen khaki slacks and short sleeve shirts, over which he could pull on wool sweaters. He picked heavy leather boots with comfy wool socks. He wore a wide-brimmed sand coloured pith helmet. It was considered wise to wear cover against the sun then. The fashion changed in the war, when men went bareheaded except for steel helmets.

He packed a kitbag full with shorts, spare underwear, socks, and shirts. He strapped on his belt and revolver holster. 'Well, off we go.' He clattered down the stairs and across the hall. The servant at the door leapt to his feet, and, taking the bag from Cecil's hand, preceded him down the outside steps to a big Ford lorry. It had large, fat, balloon, desert tyres and was loaded to the gills with petrol tins, known as flimsies, spare tyres lashed to the sides, large containers of what he surmised was water, and all kinds of packs and bundles piled one on top of another, all lashed down with tight straps and ropes.

"Morning Paynter. Ready to be off?" It was Thompson sitting at the wheel, a pipe gripped in his teeth, the smoke wreathing his face in a kind of aromatic mystery. "We decided to come and get you. Hope that's alright?"

"Good morning sir. Of course. Good of you to do that. Good morning." Cecil nodded to the other occupants, one, a tough-looking, red-faced sergeant (he had his stripes sewn on his jumper), the other two, young, fresh-faced men who both grinned and nodded.

Cecil squeezed in next to Thompson.

"All set sir."

Thompson drove with concentrated determination. As he negotiated the outskirts of Cairo, they passed the Mena House Hotel and the Pyramids and Sphinx. Ahead lay the road to the open desert.

Hours later they were pounding along a rough desert track. The road had disappeared. It was high noon. The sun burnt fiercely. Cecil was dying for a drink of water, but as none of the others had mentioned it, he didn't want to be the first, so he suffered quietly.

"Anyone like a drink?" It was Thompson.

'Thank God.'

"Wouldn't mind sir. It was the tough sergeant.

"Right. We'll stop for a bit."

They were in a shallow *wadi*, a dried up stream bed that had probably not seen moisture since before the old kings of Egypt had been born.

Thompson parked in the lee of a rock that was twice the size of the truck. Everyone piled out. Some relieved themselves. They all stretched. The sergeant, who was also the cook, began to prepare the midday meal. It was very simple and amounted to corned beef sandwiches and a cup of tepid tea with evaporated milk. They sat around and smoked and talked. The two young men were lieutenants in the Royal Engineers. Their expertise was in mapping and navigation. Their presence in the undertaking was to make sightings and notes for the report that would come out of the expedition. The principal object was to see if the area was suitable for military traffic, both wheeled and tracked.

They continued on. The desert was, in parts, like that of the romantic ideal, that is, billowing hills of sand, golden, rippling, ever-changing. Mostly though, it was flattish and of a gravel-like consistency, the odd scrubby thorn bush here and there, and otherwise, without vegetation of any sort. The horizon moved and shimmered constantly, the infamous mirage being just that: an illusion of glinting water, as of a gigantic lake, always just out of reach, disappearing as one got closer.

The enormity and the silence of it all repelled and fascinated at the same time. At night, which comes with an uncanny suddenness, the sun is at one moment a great orange ball, low down in the sky, then, gone the next moment. For only a moment there is a pale afterglow, the colour of a blackbird's egg, a pale blue-green, then darkness, but not an unilluminated darkness, for then the brilliance of the stars appears. The southern horizon is dominated by the Southern Cross above all, the great constellation glowing and coruscating.

Lying in his bedroll, Cecil gazed, entranced. They had all had a couple of glasses of whiskey and he was feeling rather pleasant. This celestial entertainment was an additional pleasure. He sighed, turned over, and went to sleep.

Next morning after a breakfast of small Arabic hen's eggs, boiled over the camp fire and eaten with a chunk of bread and a cup of tea, they set out on a compass bearing that would lead them through the Quattara Depression. This would be an important part of the excursion. Cairo Headquarters was anxious to find out if it was navigable by mobile forces. It wasn't. More records were annotated and the journey continued.

They had now reached the northern edge of the Great Sand Sea. That night they camped, knowing that they were at the limit of their endurance. This was as far as they could go. They sat after a dinner of boiled rice, cold corned beef, and mustard pickles. Dessert was a slab of bread and treacle. All was washed down by the inevitable cup of tea. Afterwards they sat and smoked. They were quieter than usual. The immensity of the surroundings was awe inspiring. All knew that there was virtually nothing living or moving between them and a French Foreign Legion Fort to their south and west, a distance of some hundreds of miles. South and south east there was nothing for perhaps a thousand miles or more to some obscure little village in the Darfur region of the Sudan. It was a savage unforgiving area of burnt sand and rock, peopled by inhospitable, nomadic tribes, dangerous in the extreme. Thompson broke the silence.

"Well Paynter, we didn't use any of your linguistic skills this time."

"No sir. Sorry sir. "

"Not your fault, When we return tomorrow we shall swing further east. Lots of camps and oases that way. You can talk your head off then."

"Yes sir. Thank you sir."

"Right. Well. let's turn in. Early start in the morning."

Cecil found it difficult to sleep that night and woke early, before the sun was up. He got up and dressed, then wandered off to perform the necessary ablutions of the morning. As he cleared a high pile of rocks and boulders he saw a light, a flickering, moving light. It was still dark so whatever it was, showed clearly against the surrounding blackness.

'What the hell can this be so far from anywhere?' Arabs never used lights of any kind when moving, so the presence of Bedou could be discounted. 'Better get back and wake the others.'

This he did and now they were clustered behind the rocks looking at Thompson who was using their one pair of binoculars and carrying out a kind of commentary. It was light now and the sun was starting to burn behind their knees. Cecil, out of the corner of his eye, watched a scorpion skitter across a rock and disappear into a crevice.

"Yes," said Thompson, "it's a lorry. Looks Italian. Yes, it's a Fiat. Two white men, and, hold it, looks like a woman. Good God! A woman here? Extraordinary. Whatever next? Well they are probably Jerries. I've heard they are about.

Better they don't see us. Back to the truck. Lets let caution be our guide."

They ran back to the vehicle that the sergeant had already started up. They piled aboard.

"Off we go Rogers. Not tooo fast don't want to raise the dust." They crawled down the *wadi*, and finding the empty desert flat as a pancake, drove steadily and dustless to the East.

They reached, that night, a small Arab encampment, parked nearby, and walked over to the tents. As was the form of polite arrival, they were greeted *"salaam alaekum,"* and replied *"alaekum salaam. Fuddle, fuddle,"* the last words indicating to make oneself at home.

They were invited to sit down and were offered *gah-wa*, the sweet, heavy Turkish coffee served in tiny cups with a sliver of lemon rind. Thompson passed his Turkish cigarettes around. They were plucked by horny, boney, brown fingers from his package. The Bedou loved to smoke. The air was soon grey with aromatic clouds. They talked.

'Had they seen the strangers?'

'Yes.'

'And who were they?'

'Not Ingleezi. There was a *Bint*, a girl.'

'Yes. Quite, quite.' This from Thompson.

They finished their cigarettes, stood up, and politely requested permission to leave. Cecil noticed they hadn't been invited to have dinner and sensed a desire on the part of their hosts to have them leave. He wondered why.

Cairo was reached two days later. they had a short

meeting at headquarters and were dispersed to their respective units, Cecil back to police HQ, where he was greeted by a chorus of friendly chaff mostly of a highly disrespectful and scatological nature. A big night out was planned for the coming weekend to celebrate his return The year was 1932. The time that he had been out east had flown by.

FUN AND GAMES...

Cecil had kept up an intermittent correspondence with his family and friends at home. He had a couple of letters from Rowena, friendly but cool. Those two days and nights on the island seemed like a dream. 'Messed that one up,' he thought. He hardly ever thought about Susan, the nurse in France. Probably married and settled down with hordes of children on some farm in the prairies of Canada. 'Oh well. She was sweet though'. He struggled with his bow tie.

Tonight was the night out. Evening dress was the celebratory standard: cummerbund of crimson silk, all decorations on left breast of mess kit, black with edges of black ribbon, trousers the same, tight and uncomfortable, but very smart, the whole topped off, literally, by a scarlet tasselled Fez. There was a tap at the door.

"Come in," he shouted. It was Nigel, who was joining them that night, and who he had not seen for several weeks.

"How are you dear boy?"

"Very well, thanks Nigel."

"Hear you were out in the Blue with Thompson last week. Have fun?"

"Certainly did. He's quite a character."

They strolled down the stairs and went out into the

scented warm darkness of the Cairo night, crossed the pavement, and climbed into a horse-drawn *gharry*. Nigel asked the driver to take them to the Shepheard Hotel. They clopped through the teeming streets, smells of cooking and throbbing drumming, wailing music, assailed their nostrils and their ears. 'God! I really am beginning to like this place,' thought Cecil.

The bar at the hotel was, as always, crowded. They threaded their way to the bar.

"Two gin and its. No ice please."

"Oh, hadn't you heard? an older, ruddy-faced silver-haired. gentleman in a white tuxedo jacket, which usually meant an American, said, looking up from his place at the bar, "Gin and its are now officially known as martinis. One of my countrymen coined the name last week. You Limeys better get used to it."

"Oh really," drawled Cecil. "They will always be gin and its to me." He turned away and said, "Bloody yanks. Think they own the world."

"Oh don't be so stuck up," said Nigel. "I've just met a rather dishy American girl. I rather like her and I think she likes me so you musn't say anything horrid about them."

"Oh Christ," said Cecil. "What next. You know Mother will die."

"Yes, I suppose so. Haven't told her yet though."

In came the gang from the station. They were all several sheets to the wind.

"God!" said Cecil. "We had better go somewhere else before they throw us out."

"But I've not finished my drink, and Charlie from Barclay's Bank was going to meet us here. Tell you what old boy," said Nigel, "I'll take them to Lulus. You stay and finish your drink and join us later."

"Alright. Sounds good. See you later."

Nigel about-turned a rather bewildered and definitely inebriated group of police officers and marched them out of the room. Cecil returned to the bar. The American swung around at his approach and said, rather unexpectedly,

"Hello darling."

Cecil, after a second of quite righteous surprise, realised that the American was addressing someone behind him, someone who smelt of Chanel. He turned around. She was tall, blonde, and quite stunning. She regarded him without interest and swept by.

"Hello my sweet." She and the American embraced.

"Meet my Limey friend," the American said, nodding towards Cecil. "What's your name buddy?"

Cecil told him.

"Jesus Christ! You're kidding."

The girl smiled faintly. Cecil tried to look dignified and succeeded in appearing slightly ridiculous instead.

"Really," he said sounding pompous, "I can't think why you should say that. It's a perfectly respectable English name."

"You're telling me," said the American. "Anyway, have a drink. What'll you have?"

"Er, I'll have a gin and it. Oh, okay. You win. Martini"

"George," he motioned to the bar tender who was

hovering within earshot. "You heard that?"

"Yessir. Coming right up."

"So, what brings you to Cairo?" Cecil asked the girl who was sitting quietly sipping champagne.

"I'm an archeologist. Actually we're doing some digs in the south near the Quattara."

"Oh, really?" said Cecil. "How very interesting. Where are you from? I hear an accent."

"She's a countess. You be nice to her," the American interjected.

"Good God!" said Cecil. "In what country?"

"Austria," she answered. "My name is Wanda."

The American said, "She's doing hush, hush work really."

"Oh, do shut up Miles," she snapped, obviously annoyed. She looked quickly at Cecil who pretended disinterest.

"Shall we go somewhere else? It's a bit quiet here. I feel like doing the town."

At that moment Cecil's friend from Barclays Bank walked in.

"Hello Tom. Come and have a drink with us. Then we're going to Lulu's."

"That sounds like fun. Can I join you?" said Tom, shaking hands with Cecil and the American, but looking at the Countess.

"Of course dear boy. The rest of the lads are there."

One more round appeared and was polished off. Cecil paid the bill and turned to join the others. He noticed Tom attentively helping with a wrap, placing it on shapely shoulders. 'Cheeky bugger,' thought Cecil. She seemed to be enjoying the attention though, and was looking up at Tom with interest. 'Damn!' They all piled into a *gharry* and went to one of the best known cabarets in the city.

Lulu was a French woman of unknown years who had adopted Cairo as her home. She had been running the place for years and was beloved of the fast crowd. No one knew her last name or where in France she came from. It was said that she had opened a bar in Sidi bel Abbas, the French Foreign Legion town in Algeria and had made a small fortune smuggling booze. She was run out of town by the authorities and had come to Egypt with her takings and started the establishment they were now entering.

One went through a large hall that had seen better days: the walls peeling stucco that had been patchily repaired and painted. The woodwork was a faded blue-green, marked and scratched by time and spilt wine, the waxed tile of the floor gleamed, but was chipped and worn and stained. The whole effect was of slightly decayed splendour. There were three doors and an open archway. The doors led, one to an upstairs office, Lulu's den, the other two, to rooms of comfort for ladies and gentlemen.

They proceeded through the arched door that led to an open area of tables and chairs surrounded by a high mimosa-covered wall, a stage at one side of the space, on which an Arab jazz band played in a dissonant but not unattractive manner. The place was packed. White-clad waiters with turbans and green cummerbunds rushed about with food and drink. It was lit by strings of coloured light bulbs that hung from cedar trees that stood about.

The waiter led them to a table close to the band and took their order, which was simple: Champagne, except for Wanda who ordered, with a mischievous grin, a Champagne cocktail.

"That's a bit adventurous isn't it?" said Cecil.

"Well I'm feeling adventurous." She laughed and looked him in the eye for a long languorous moment that left him shaky but excited.

"Darling, order some champers," she spoke to Miles.

"I want to dance with Cecil before the cabaret begins."

"Sure. Okay honey. Will do."

"Come on you, you Englishman, let's see what you've got."

She took him by the hand and led him to the crowded floor. The band was playing a slow, melodic, sensuous, tango number. She turned and melted into Cecil's arms. Her body pressed into his as she clasped him around the neck, and, gazing up into his eyes, moved to the music. Cecil tried to follow her but without too much luck. 'This is all too much,' he thought, especially as he was starting to feel a definite reaction to the movements of her body.

"Oh dear." she said smiling up at him. "I think you and I had better leave."

"Yes, I think that would be a good idea. I'm terribly sorry. I'm so embarrassed."

"My dear, don't apologise. I think it's wonderful."

Cecil was in such ecstasy that the ride in the *gharry* back to the hotel went by as if in a dream. He was, as was common in those days, quite inexperienced in matters of a sexual nature. For English men of that class and age the matter never came up. It just was not done. It was like money. One didn't have much to do with it, or talk about it. His previous experiences with Rowena and Susan had been largely a matter of the incentive being taken by the female with his contribution amounting to some very clumsy thrusting, the whole business being over in seconds. His education in these matters however, was about to begin.

The sheets were cool and felt like satin. Her body was warm and felt like silk. Her scent, a wonderful, almost indescribable aroma of sandalwood, musk, and something else, something indefinable. It was as though spells were being cast, and magic made. Cecil kissed her gently, her eyes, her cheek, mouth, and neck, her shoulders and her breasts. She caressed his face and lips and kissed him softly and openly. He felt the thrill of her searching, arching body and began to respond. She sighed and moved under him. Heaven was here. Heaven was now. Heaven was his.

The breeze at dawn moved the mosquito curtain that sheltered them. A faint scent of frangipani drifted in from the gardens. Cecil opened his eyes and looked at her lovely face. With her eyes closed she looked like a child. He put his hand out and stroked her face.

She smiled and said "My darling, is it time to get up?"

They left the hotel separately. Discretion was valued

then, reputations important, honour paramount.

The call from his headquarters came as a shock, the peremptory manner and tone was disturbing.

"Paynter! Get over here at once!" It was *Bimbashi* Ferguson.

'God. What was up?' He struggled into his uniform glancing at his watch. He saw that he had slept until noon, but it was his day off duty so he wasn't worried about being tardy. He grabbed a taxi.

"Police Headquarters, Sharia Al Mansour." The driver crashed the gears in a hurry to be off. Cecil's head reeled. Too much champagne and not enough sleep: neither his mind nor body were exactly in the best of health.

They screeched up to the offices next to the Grand Continental Hotel. He paid the cab and ran as quickly as he could up the steps. 'Hope I can get a cup of coffee before I see them,' he thought. No such luck.

The duty sergeant at the desk looked up and said anxiously, "Oh, Mr. Payne, Sir, you must go right in. *Bimbashi* Ferguson urgently wants to see you. Go right in."

Cecil tapped at the door.

"Come in," a voice roared.

"You wanted to see me sir?" Cecil said meekly.

"Bloody right I want to see you!" Ferguson's face was scarlet, his expression indicating imminent apoplexy. "You can't do anything in Cairo without me knowing about it. Are you aware who you were sleeping with last night?"

"Of course sir. She is an Austrian countess, with, I

believe, impeccable credentials in archeology."

"Well you're partly right. She is an archeologist, but she's not Austrian and she is certainly not a countess. She's actually German and she's working for the bad boys. They are doing the same things as we are, checking out the lay of the land in case the balloon goes up. The bloody Italians are making a bloody nuisance of themselves on the Somali-Abyssinian border. The whole area is in a state of tension. She was probably hoping you would spill a few tasty morsels she could pass back to Berlin. Christ man. You were sleeping with the opposition!"

"I assure you sir nothing of importance was discussed. The whole evening was innocent, in that respect."

"All right Paynter. I believe you. I know you're a reasonable chap. Just wanted to make sure. You will, of course, not see the lady again, and just to make sure we are sending you to Khartoum for a week or two. Go and see what's going on with the Italians and the Abyssinians. You can liaise with the lads in Khartoum. All right. Off you go."

TO SUDAN...

The great Scottish-made locomotive steamed and clanked at the head of the long buff-coloured train as it stood in the terminus at Cairo waiting for the whistle that would start it off on its journey south to Aswan. Cecil had just arrived in time to buy some magazines and find his sleeping compartment, which was in a coach near the front, so he had to run the length of the train and closed the door just as the locomotive gave its first hoot to be off.

The train gave a jerk and started to move. A breath of air came through the open shuttered window. The fan revolving above his head picked it up and began to distribute it about the cabin. He lit a cigarette. 'This is nice,' he thought. Memories about the last train journey when he had met Rowena and her father, began to percolate. 'I wonder how she is? I must write.'

He pondered the future. He was, first of all, looking forward to the trip itself. These were the railway lines that had carried many of General Kitchener's troops to the south to fight the Khalifa Abdullahi and his Dervish Army at places like Atbara, and eventually the great battle at Omdurman. The train would take him to Aswan where he would change to a stern-wheel paddle boat which would go to the first Nile Cataract, the first of six virtually impassable rapids of the great river.

Then they went back to the train, over the unimaginable desert across the Central Sudan, the enormous, unforgiving, dangerous, desert. 'When Allah made the Sudan, he laughed,' the locals said bitterly. Some many hours later he would arrive at Khartoum, the capital of this strange, vast, and savage land.

The assignment he had been given should be interesting. It would be a salutary experience to work with the Sudanese Police and with the Nilotic tribes they dealt with: the Nubian of the southern marshes and bush, as well as the Arab Nomad of the central and northern provinces, with their Bisharin racing camels, fleet, bad-tempered and vociferous, and the Baggara with their wild horses, as well as with the Fuzzy Wuzzy of the Red Sea Hills, the Hadendoa and Beja, the descendants of those that broke the regimental squares in all those blood-soaked skirmishes in that River War of so long ago.

The heat in the compartment coupled with the drinks he had in Cairo conspired to put him to sleep. It was dark when he woke. He glanced at his watch. 'Good God!' It was six o'clock. He had slept for three hours. The train was clacking along, swaying and bumping. He made his way to the little attached room which held a tilting metal basin on gimbels, waiting to be filled with tepid water from a jug. He washed his face and hands, and felt better.

He realised that he felt hungry as well as thirsty. He knew there was a dining car somewhere on the train and decided to try to find it.

"Good evening sir. Table for one?" The captain smiled and motioned him to a table.

He sat and looked out at the darkening sky, then at the menu. He'd heard the food was good on this train.

"Something to drink?" A uniformed Sudanese steward hovered.

"Yes, thanks. A gin and tonic I think. A double."

"Right sir. Right away."

Cecil looked about him. The saloon was quite full, some obviously tourists from their clothes and manner: American and rich; some uniformed people, brown, lean, and relaxed, almost too relaxed. They had been drinking to excess by the sound of them. A few that were hard to identify, but were, by the look of them, old Africa hands, probably working at something just on the wrong side of the law, gun-running, ivory poaching, or perhaps just innocent safari guides. Whatever they were, they all looked as though they knew what life was all about.

The drink arrived, and with it the steward to take his order. He chose a soup he had been told about called *ful Sudani* consisting of peanuts crushed and cooked in some sort of broth with copious amounts of herbs and spices. It turned out to be delicious. For the main course he had Nile Perch, probably caught that day. He took a sip of gin and lit a cigarette, relaxed and content.

The sound of hooting awoke him next morning. It didn't sound like the train locomotive, which had the quality of a tooting whistle. This was deeper, more like a foghorn. 'Of course!' They had arrived at Aswan. That was the noise a ship makes. It was the river boat. 'Oh, this was exciting!'

He called for a porter and soon found himself climbing aboard the boat, preceded by his luggage, which was perched delicately on the heads of two porters. The craft was called Bordein 2. He remembered his history. The first Bordein was one of General Gordon's boats at Khartoum in 1888. This one was quite large with massive paddles at the stern, an extensive superstructure, one big funnel, and two stubby masts. The upper decks were busy with natives running about pulling on ropes, stacking deck cargo, and trying to keep out of the way of gawking passengers, the tourists he had noticed on the train. His cabin was found and his suitcases were deposited.

This was going to be his home for the next several hours. The boat would sail that afternoon for the town of Dongola, some 500 miles to the south, a couple of days, he estimated.

By the time he'd settled in and unpacked, the morning had fled. 'Ah, time for a quick one before lunch' he thought. The lounge and bar were located on the upper deck astern of the funnel. It was already crowded with thirsty passengers. He worked his way to a table, at which sat two young men in the uniform of the Sudan Camel Corps, identifiable by their black buttons and insignia, and the huge black ostrich feathers attached to the up-turned brim of their hats.

"May I sit down?"

"Of course old boy. Sit you down." An unmistakable Irish accent. "Will you have a drink with us, though what my old dad would say about me drinking with an English policeman, cannot be imagined." He grinned and held out his hand.

Cecil took it.

"It's alright. My mother came from Greystones."

"Ah, that's alright then. Meet my chum Alan Morris. He's a Jock." Greetings were exchanged.

At that moment some drinks arrived, gin slings by the look of them.

"Bring another please. So what's an Egyptian copper doing going south?"

Cecil told them what he could without giving too much away.

"Oh, very interesting. We've had patrols all up and down the borders with the Ities. There's been a lot of activity on their side."

"D'you think trouble's coming?"

"Don't know. Shouldn't think so. They've got their hands full with the Abyssinians who will be tough for them to keep down. No, from what I hear it's the bloody Germans who are getting bloody-minded and they are a long way from here."

"Yes. Suppose you're right."

"Well, should be moving soon. Hell-oo! What a corker. His already red face got suddenly redder and his eyes lit up. He was looking at someone or something behind Cecil. Cecil swung round.

A tall, quite stunningly beautiful young woman was approaching them. She was walking with some older people, who Cecil had noticed earlier as possible American tourists. She was engrossed with something an elegant silver-haired man was telling her. As they passed, she looked at Cecil and smiled. Cecil was transfixed.

A loud bellow from the funnel's siren sounded. Billowing brown smoke issued upwards and blotted out the sun. Thrashing noises of the paddles beginning to revolve in the water astern joined in the cacophony.

"Let's go up top," he said to the two officers.

"Good idea, old boy."

They climbed the companion way to the upper deck and looked around. The boat was puffing away from the jetty and had almost reached centre stream. It was midday and the sun was burning in a glaring white sky.

"Well, I think I've had enough of the great outdoors. Shall we repair to the bar for a drink before lunch?" This was Jock.

"Dangerous not to," said the Irishman. "Lead on MacDuff."

Drinks led to lunch which was that dish taken by Great Britain from the kitchens of India, kedgeree, a curried mélange of smoked fish, rice, and eggs, often served throughout the hottest parts of the Empire at high noon, usually accompanied with sliced bananas, almonds, and cucumbers, with, of course, masses of chutney and lots of India Pale Ale to wash it all down. A really eccentric dessert, steamed syrup pudding, followed. Then, an afternoons siesta of some length ensued.

Waking up was difficult. First of all, Cecil was dreaming about the ravishing beauty he had seen earlier, and secondly, more lager had been consumed at lunch than was wise. He tottered to the wash basin and threw water in his face, brushed his teeth and hair, flicked his shoes with a cloth, and walked out into the cooling Egyptian evening. He was facing west, so was confronted by a subtropical sunset at its full apogee. The sky was livid with alternate streaks of pink, yellow, orange, and darkening grey. A sliver of sun remained, but as he watched, it slipped behind the horizon. 'God!' he thought. 'I need a drink after that.' He quickly made his way to the bar.

"Well about time. You look like hell!" It was his new Irish friend, "You've just missed The Goddess. She asked about you. She's coming back."

"Good Lord, did she? What did she say?"

"Oh this and that. She fancies you that's for sure."

"What'll you have."

"Oh, beer I think. I'm thirsty." He looked about. The bar was bright with light and activity. Outside, darkness had fallen. Funny, tomorrow I'll be back on a train again, the last part of the journey from Dongola to Khartoum. I've gotten rather fond of the old boat. His thoughts were interrupted by the Irishman again.

"Uh oh. Here she comes. Sort yourself out."

"Oh, hello," The Goddess spoke.

"Oh, er, hello," answered Cecil, lamely.

"Will you buy me a drink?"

"Of course." She had to be American. No self-respecting young English girl would be so forth-coming. And Cecil thought it charming. "Yes of course. Er, ah, what will you have." He cursed his clumsiness and lack of confidence.

"I'd like what you're having."

"What, a beer?"

"Yes."

He liked her even more.

"What are you doing here, touring with your family?"

"No, they're my flock. I'm a tour guide. We're going to the southern Sudan and to Northern Kenya. She pronounced it Keenya, the old way. "They want to photograph wild life. I believe there are white rhino galore."

"Yes, that's right," interjected the Irishman, "also all sorts of gazelle, tommies, ibex, lion, and yaws."

"Yaws?" the girl said, puzzled. "What are yaws?"

"I'll have a gin and tonic," laughed Paddy, taking the cue from his set-up.

They all smiled.

"It wasn't that funny," said Cecil, miffed, wanting to keep her all to himself. He need not have worried. She turned away from Ireland and concentrated her attention on Cecil. It was quite unnerving. The dinner gong was ringing.

"Would you keep me company?" she asked, looking at Cecil meaningfully. "Just you?"

"Of course. Delighted."

"Okay. I can take a hint. See you later. Behave children." Paddy drank up, dropped some money on the bar, and left.

Her name was Isabel. She came from the city of New York from a family that sounded as though they might have money and status. She had gone to all the best schools, loved to travel, and was something of an expert on the tribes of East Africa, where she had lived in some discomfort and danger amongst the people she was studying.

They ate and laughed and drank and laughed. They were beside themselves with pleasure at being together. She was lovely, and he was falling in love. Her utter indifference to the rules of the class he came from, charmed him. She looked at the world around her with an openness and lightheartedness that was at once appealing and impressive. They held hands across the table and gazed into each others eyes.

"More wine dear?"

"No. I want you to make love to me. Let's go to your cabin."

There are many wonderful and exciting places to make love, but it would be hard to find anywhere as romantic as a stern-wheeled paddleboat on the upper Nile going south under the stars.

Sadly, the time came for them to end this idyllic and magical voyage. The old boat came to dock at Dongola and bags and baggage were unloaded and placed into a waiting train. The passengers followed. Isabel and her group were being met by a safari guide who had a pair of Ford A trucks waiting. They were going west to Darfur, before they proceeded to Khartoum. This was goodbye, for at least the time being. They embraced.

"Call me when you get to town," said Cecil gruffly. "You'll find me through the police HQ."

"Yes darling. I will. God, this is awful." Tears welled.

Cecil kissed her wet cheek.

"Yes. Take good care of her." He said, feeling a bit lost

and sad, while speaking to the Americans standing by the cars.

"We will. She's very precious to us too."

"Right. Well, goodbye." He turned on his heel and strode to the train, blinking his eyes.

The time in the train fortunately was relatively short. Cecil was deflated, and felt empty. Somehow the excitement of the trip and the prospects ahead seemed less appealing. He missed Isabel terribly already. Somehow the day passed. Evening came. Dinner was consumed. Nothing tasted right. Even the couple of drinks before dinner didn't cheer. Conversation with his new friends was without interest. Sleep came as some relief, but was troubled by dreams of a disturbing nature.

Introductions...

A change in the sound of the wheels on the tracks woke him. He leaned up and pulled the blind open. It was early, just getting light. They were crossing a bridge. This was where the track crossed the Nile. Here, the river separated the great, sprawling, ancient, native city of Omdurman from the more European, somewhat modernised city of Khartoum, which means, in Arabic, elephant's trunk. A look at a map will explain.

"Mr. Paynter?" A tall officer in the uniform of the Sudanese Police Force approached and saluted.

"Yes? Good morning."

"Good morning sir. My name is Manners. I'm to take you to HQ. The car's over here." He motioned to the parking area. "Mohamed will take your bags."

A very black Sudani constable saluted, grinned whitely, and, picking Cecil's luggage, walked to where a sand-coloured vehicle waited.

"Good trip sir?"

"Yes, very good. Nice to be back on terra firma though."

"Yes, quite," Manners chuckled. "It's quite the journey. Oops, lookout Mohamed. Don't want to knock anyone over."

The car was being driven by the constable who seemed

to delight in just missing pedestrians in the crowded streets. As well as people on foot there were strings of small donkeys all roped together with a young lad waving a stick on the leading animal. Impassive camels, chewing and indifferent, loped along as though they owned the road. Their riders were dusty, but proud-looking.

Cecil noticed some were armed, some with rifles and some with elegant swords slung over their shoulders, an odd antiquated look completely out of keeping with the motor car traffic that crowded the streets, hooting and honking. Cecil wondered about the rules that might or might not apply to the bearing of arms.

Leading to the area around the station, the car swept onto a broad tree-lined avenue that apparently led to the centre of the city. Cecil gazed about, entranced by all the activity and newness of the surroundings.

"Here we are. HQ."

They had pulled up at an official-looking building, over which flew both the flag of Egypt and of Great Britain, reflecting the fact that, officially, both countries ruled the Sudan. The arrangement was known as the Anglo-Egyptian Condominium.

Cecil followed Manners up the steps. A sentry at the door snapped off a salute, coming to attention and slapping the rifle butt smartly.

It was cool and dark inside the hallway and smelt like it does in a school, a mixture of sharpened pencils, waxed floors, and musty paper. Manners led the way through a set of glass doors and into a long corridor lined with doorways that accessed other offices. He tapped on one door with a brass lettered plate on it that read "*Kaimakan* Roberts" a voice inside said "come in" and they did.

Inside it was all sunlight and brightness. After the dark hallway they had just left, the change was startling, and Cecil had to blink a couple of times to accustom himself to the light.

It was a large room full of furniture: desks, file cabinets, chairs. Piles of papers and books lay everywhere. The walls held framed sepia photographs of sporting, school, and regimental groups. A large collection of silver competitive cups and medals occupied a table in the corner. A big man strode around the desk to greet him.

"How do you do? Welcome to the Sudan. I hope Manners has looked after you alright?"

"Oh yes Sir. Very well, thank you."

"Right. Well. What shall we do with you? How about a little trip into the hills on the border, eh what? See what the Ities are up to. Would you take him Manners? You can check on that little bit of trouble the local Bejas stirred up at Gallabat last week while you're there, what?"

"Of course sir."

"Right then. So off you go."

"Could I take Tony Price with me sir? He needs some time out in the blue."

"Oh Tony. Yes. That's a good idea. D'you think he'll go?"

"Oh I think I can persuade him."

"Good, good. Excellent. Now where are my glasses? I

know they are here somewhere." He fumbled absentmindedly on the desk.

"What an old dear," said Cecil.

"Yes, he's rather a sweetheart. But don't kid yourself. When things get rough Bob's in there with the best of them."

"Who's Tony Price?"

"Oh he's our resident aristocrat. Son of a lord. He's an Hon, actually. He's okay really. Bit full of himself at times. You'll like him. Loves to party. You'll meet him at mess tonight."

Cecil spent the rest of the day resting. He hadn't realised how tired he was after the journey he had just undertaken. He collapsed on the bed without bothering to fix the mosquito netting, and was soon fast asleep.

It was almost dark when he awoke. Glancing at his watch he saw that he had an hour to dress for dinner. There was a tap at the door.

"Come in." A very tall, very black police constable holding a uniform and shoes came in.

"Your uniform sir. All cleaned and pressed. Shoes all shiny. All ready sir."

"But where did all this come from? How did you get my clothes?"

"Oh me fix sir. I unpack all your kit while you sleep sir. All okay sir?" His face wrinkled anxiously.

"Oh yes. Very okay. Thank you so much constable."

Thank you sah." The plum black face split into a great white shiny grin. "My name Ahmed sah. You call when you need anything."

A cool shower restored spirits, and getting into a crisp white shirt and dress uniform added to the pleasure. He tipped the Fez to just the right angle: 'not too jaunty, can't look flashy. Okay, off we go.'

He descended the stairs to the main room, which was already full of uniformed officers. Some elegantly dressed women were about, probably wives of the few civilian guests present. *Suffragis*, uniformed servants in white robes with green cummerbunds threaded their ways through the throng, carrying trays with drinks and canapés. One approached Cecil, who took a glass of white wine and looked around, sipping.

"Hello Paynter. Have a good rest?" It was his chief, Roberts. "That's right. Have a drink and come and meet some people. Mr. and Mrs. Valsamides, this is *Bimbashi* Paynter, visiting from Cairo."

"How do you do Mr. Paynter." She was dark and exotic and held out her hand in a manner that invited a kiss. This Cecil did. A languorous perfume emanated from her. Her husband was not so forthcoming, confining his greeting to a brief nod. From the name, Cecil presumed they were Greek. He was some sort of trader, and from the look of her jewellery, a successful one. Other people came up to be introduced, and Cecil found himself the centre of attention as the guest of the evening.

A long bibulous night followed. The food was excellent, as was the wine. Both were consumed in copious quantities. He met the infamous Tony Price, who was friendly, handsome, and quite tight. Cecil knew that they would become great pals in no time. Other people came into and out of Cecil's ken. The night went by in a whirling, enjoyable blur.

RECONNAISSANCE...

The morning came too soon. Today they were to begin the trip to the border. They had made the arrangements during one of the few relatively sober periods of the night before.

Cecil bathed and shaved and dressed. 'Khaki drill, Sam Brown belt, holstered revolver, binoculars, sun helmet, compass. Oops. Need a clean hankie. Right. Breakfast I think.'

"Morning Paynter. How d'yer feel?"

"Not bad, considering. How about you?"

"Ghastly. Too much gin I'm afraid."

Cecil helped himself from the sideboard on which breakfast was laid: scrambled eggs and bacon, grilled tomatoes, and, maybe, yes, lovely fried bread. He took the plate to where there was an empty chair and sat down. There was almost as much food on the table. Jars of jams, marmalades, racks of toast, pots of tea and coffee, all steaming away, all being consumed by hungry young men. He tucked in.

They all smoked a cigarette with their last cup of coffee, and when finished, those that were going with Cecil got up patting their lips with napkins.

"Well, shall we pop off?" This was Manners.

"Absolutely. I'm ready." A rather hung-over-looking Tony Price spoke up.

"Good. Roberts?" Manners looked at the other member of the party, a young subaltern who Cecil had spoken to briefly at dinner and who had apparently just come out from England, and who was looking nervously at his shoes.

"Oh, er, yes sir. Ready here sir."

"Alright, alright. I'm not going to eat you. We're all friends here. Right off we go."

They all trooped outside. It was already blazing hot. There were three vehicles parked by the steps, the motor cars of choice in those parts: two Ford As painted sand yellow with canvas tops, and a light Ford lorry piled with lashed-down boxes and canvas bags. Two grinning Sudani *Askaris* were sitting on top. Three other black constables sat at the wheels, looking pleased with themselves. Cecil found himself sitting with Manners in one car. The other two disposed themselves in the second.

With much crashing of gears and revving of engines they began the long journey that would take two days and two nights and would go due east across the flat, dry, stony, inhospitable eastern Sudan, and would, if all went well, bring them to the border with Italian-occupied Eritrea and the town of Kassala.

Cecil studied the map unfolded on his knees and found their first stopping place the town of Wad Medani. ETA he reckoned would be some time tomorrow. He lit a cigarette and sat back. Closing his eyes, he thought about the last few hectic days. He had just started to dream about Isabel when reality interrupted.

"Christ! What the hell was that? Ouch!" His finger burned.

"God Paynter don't burn the car up. You went to sleep for a second." Manners was laughing. "Here. I'll move over a bit. Put your head down. Get some sleep."

"Oh thanks Sir. I could use some shut-eye."

The first thing of which Cecil was aware after that was being shaken awake and realising that the car was stopped and that it was pitch dark.

"Feel better?"

"Thank you sir. I do."

"Abdullah has set up washing facilities. You'll feel even better after a wash."

"Yes, thank you." Cecil headed over to where some metal bowls had been placed on a collapsible table, took off his shirt and threw tepid water over his head and face. A good scrub with yellow kitchen soap helped get rid of some of the dust. 'Phew. That's better.'

He turned towards the group sitting by a fire that crackled and snapped near the tents. It dawned on him then, that while he'd been sleeping a complete camp had been set up. There was a pleasant aroma of something cooking. A billy can bubbling and steaming hung over the fire.

"Like a drink Cecil?" It was the lord's son.

"You bet!" Some whiskey was poured into a dusty glass and handed to him.

"Mmm." He downed it in one draft and handed the glass back. "More please."

"Right," said Tony grinning.

Later they sat and ate what Abdullah had cooked. It was some kind of stew with a gamey flavour. Cecil guessed it was some sort of desert gazelle, which were common in the area and often hunted for food. This was cooked in a broth with potatoes, carrots, and spiced with some sort of herb that he couldn't recognise.

"It's cumin," said Tony.

"What?"

"It's cumin. The taste you can't identify."

"Oh thanks. It's good."

"They put it in everything here," said Tony.

After supper they sat and smoked. Everyone puffed on cigarettes except Manners who favoured an old briar pipe that had seen better days and emitted great clouds of rancorous smoke. They chatted about the day's drive and the plans for tomorrow.

"We should keep a sharp lookout. We'll be going through Hadendowa country. They can get a bit frisky if roused. Also there might be some Italian patrols out. Well I'm off to bed. Up early tomorrow. 'Sparrows fart' we used to call it in France. Goodnight gentlemen."

"Goodnight sir," they spoke in unison.

Cecil, as he got sleepy, stared up at the brilliance above where even the most distant constellations could be seen looking like shimmering silver mists. A background to the closer stars that glittered and sparkled. Then he slept.

He woke next morning with the sun in his eyes and the

distinct feeling that he was being looked at. That odd feeling that comes to one sometimes and which often proves correct. He looked around.

'Dear God! What the hell is that?' An enormous yellow brown spider was sitting on the little stand that held his metal wash basin. It had large bluish blobs on the end of long antennae that swayed about, its eyes, now in the process of contemplating Cecil. The span of its hairy legs had to be at least fifteen inches or more, its body like an elliptical tennis ball. It seemed suddenly to crouch. Then with extraordinary power leaped completely across the tent, scuttled under the flap and disappeared.

Thoroughly awake now and in a state of some alarm, Cecil exited the tent and blurted out his experience to the others. Manners and Tony Price laughed.

"Sorry old boy. Should have warned you about those little beauties. Camel Spiders. Nasty bite. Worse than scorpions."

The next day after a quick breakfast they struck camp and set off into the area known as the Red Sea Hills. The landscape began to change from flattish gravel and sandy desert, to rocky undulating country, interspersed with small hills of boulders piled one on the other and rising to some hundreds of feet. The stones, some of which were enormous, were dark in colour, and from the distance looked black and ominous. Cecil heard a metallic clicking sound from behind him. The unmistakable sound of a weapon being cocked. He looked back. Tony, revolver in hand, grinned.

"Better safe than sorry, what?"

"Yes. Quite." He removed his sidearm from its holster and slipped off the safety. He looked about him. The lorry with the constables was now ahead of them and he could see them looking alertly about, their rifles at the ready.

As they rocked up and down, doing about forty across the rough ground Cecil began to feel slightly nauseated and reached around for his water bottle and an aspirin. As he was unscrewing the cap there was a loud bang.

"Christ they've hit the water skin on the lorry." Goat skin bags of water were strapped to the doors of vehicles in the desert. These were latched forward, open for cooling. The one on the lorry ahead had been pierced and was spouting water in all directions.

The vehicles skidded to a stop and slewed sideways. Estimating where the shot had come from everyone jumped out and took cover on the opposite side of the cars.

"See anyone?" It was Manners.

"No sir."

Another shot rang out. The bullet ricocheted off a rock and went singing off into space. A rattle of musketry came from the constables in front. Dust flew up from the ridge to their front and some yelling and movement took place.

"There they go," shouted Tony, as a group of fuzzy haired tribesmen scattered away down the slope, running like gazelles between and over the rocks and stones.

"Fire high over their heads Abdullah."

"Right sah," answered the grinning sergeant. The volley

crackled overhead. The would-be ambushers disappeared into the hazy distance.

"Well, a nice welcome, I must say," said Manners. "Abdullah!"

"Sah!"

"There's a village around here isn't there?"

"Yes sah."

"Right. We'll go and have a word with the Emir there. What's up Paynter? You look a bit pale."

"Yes sir. Sorry sir. Gyppy tummy, you know."

"Yes, er, quite, quite."

They mounted up and drove off, the Sudani sergeant leading the way. They travelled for about an hour. It was starting to get dark. Ahead Cecil saw lights. They turned out to be the flickering flames of a number of large cooking fires. It seemed to be quite a big village with numerous huts, which were called *tukuls*, round huts made of mud and grass. Children were still running about, although it was now quite dark. Veiled women ran after them, scolding. A small group of men, their hair frizzed up on top with great heavy ringlets hanging down behind, approached. They were all armed with broad-bladed spears. Some had strapped on over their shoulders, swords in elaborate leather scabbards. They all held little round hippopotamus skin shields, the centres of which were studded with bronze bosses. They looked formidable.

The tribe they belonged to was one of a group of related families that had fought the British Army on and off for years. These were Kipling's Fuzzy Wuzzies that broke the regimental square on several occasions. These were the ones that caused the blood-soaked desert of Newbolt's poetry. They were brave, handsome, humorous, and honest. The usual greetings took place.

"Salaam Alaikum."

"Alaikum Salaam. Ya Said. Fuddle, fuddle."

Everyone relaxed. Cecil heard the rifle bolts click behind him as they were driven home and safeties put on. The constables had been at the ready, just in case.

The tribesmen beckoned them to follow and led the way to a hut that was bigger than the others. Cecil noticed that at the back of their heads the natives all had what looked like sticks or twigs stuck in their hair. These were what he had heard of, scratching sticks. As the favoured pomade here was a mixture of camel dung and cooking oil, these implements were, no doubt, vital. Cecil also noticed a strong odour emanating from their persons. Strangely enough, it was not offensive. They wore a cotton shift over their shoulders the colour of tallow.

The hut entrance was narrow and low. Cecil had to bend down to go in, following Manners. Inside it was smoky and dim. A fire crackled briskly. Sparks and smoke climbed up and through a hole in the roof. The walls were plastered and smooth. There were three men sitting. They looked up. The rituals of recognition and hospitality were followed. They all sat down, cross-legged. Heavy black coffee was offered and accepted gratefully. Manners passed a package of Players cigarettes around. These were selected with smiles, examined carefully, and with broad grins, lit with large kitchen matches. Smoke rings were expelled. Everyone sat back in comfort and contentment.

Conversation began. Manners, through Abdullah as interpreter, asked the Chief Emir about the ambush. The chief smiled and gestured. They are just boys having a little fun. No animosity was intended. Manners grunted.

"Well, give them a talking to, someone could have been hurt or worse."

The chief smiled again and nodded. "Yes, yes."

Manners asked about the Italians. The chief really lit up at that. Yes they were around making a bloody nuisance of themselves. Apparently, they were, it seemed, arrogant and bullying. The chief hoped that the Ingleezi were here to get rid of them. Manners explained that as there were no official hostilities, nothing could be done. This elicited obvious disappointment in the faces of these old warriors, who commented that they would have to act as they saw fit with the troubling enemy. Manners said that he would look the other way and wished them luck.

Manners then stood up, and saluting all round, prepared to leave. The Emirs leapt to their feet and constrained them to stay for supper. Manners explained their hurry and they were allowed to leave with reluctance. There were salutations all round and a generous dispensation of Players which were received with great jubilation.

Later, as they were driving through the night, Manners remarked, "I think we've made good friends there. They will be useful to us when the balloon goes up. Right. Let's make camp."

ADVENTURES IN THE DESERT...

Next morning puffing on the first cigarette of the day and sipping coffee from a tin mug, Cecil checked through his diary which he had started to keep in Cairo. It came as something of a shock to realise that time had gone much faster than he could believe. It had been over ten years since he had landed in Port Said. It was now 1935, the month of August. Extraordinary how time had flown.

"All ready?" It was Manners.

"Yessir. Ready."

"Good. Let's go. We've got to make the next village by tonight."

Engines were started up and they were off, the native constables leading the way, great white grins splitting their wonderful black faces. Cecil was really beginning to like them. They were always so cheerful and willing and seemed to have no fear.

The Italians had occupied Eritrea and the world was waiting for them to invade Ethiopia. The previous winter, after some initial difficulties, they had defeated the ill-equipped and virtually untrained Eritrean Army. They now controlled much of that country.

They should, by nightfall, reach that area, but first they

had to cross several hundred miles of rough country. Though the going now was flattish, Cecil could see in the distance the smoky blue-grey of the hills that guarded the tribes of Red Sea Littoral.

Darkness fell long before they reached their destination. They had seen very little moving during the journey: a couple of desert buses overcrowded with people and livestock wallowing along on their fat desert tyres; they saw some Beja camel trains, were glared at by the tribesmen and ignored by the camels, who minced along on their soft flat feet, chewing impassively.

It was with surprise then, that ahead, in the darkness, glowing above a ridge, a light appeared. Cecil thought, 'Strange, this is a repeat of last night. Hope the stew's still hot.' The rear lights of the truck in front flickered as brakes were applied. They stopped. One of the constables in front came running back.

"What is it Ali?" asked Manners.

"Sir, the sergeant and one man are going forward on foot to see."

"Good. Well done. Abdullah knows what he's doing. Right come on Paynter lets have a *shufti*."

They jumped down. Cecil saw Manners unbuttoning his holster and tugging his sidearm out. He did the same. They trotted over to the other vehicle where the other constables stood gazing into the darkness ahead, rifles at the ready. He suddenly felt cold.

After a few minutes Abdullah came loping back. He

saluted and said, "Small camp sir. Not native people, white people sir. Not soldiers. No guards sir. Two motor cars."

"Strange," said Manners. "Who could it be? Well let's see. Don't sound too dangerous. Come on Paynter. We'll walk over. Whistle or something. Don't want to alarm them, what?" Manners actually strolled down the gully puffing away at his briar waving his walking stick in the air and commenting loudly on this and that. Cecil followed, trying not to laugh.

"Hello there. No need to get up. Just passing by. Saw your fires. Everything alright?"

The people sitting around the fire, who had jumped to their feet at the approach, looked relieved and came towards them, smiling.

"Hello, hello. Well you did give us a bit of a scare. There's been some shifty-looking characters lurking around all day. We thought they were back. We've got one rifle between us and only one of us knows how to use it. And she's a girl."

"Good God!" said Manners. "Are you Yanks?"

"Yes, as a matter of fact, we are."

At that moment another woman emerged from one of the tents. Cecil was dumbfounded. It was Isabel, the girl on the boat!

"What are you doing here?"

"Darling!" Isabel saw him and ran over. They hugged.

"What's going on?" asked Manners, who looked as though he was about to have a stroke. Even the normally unflappable Abdullah stood there with his mouth open and his eyes popping. Explanations followed. Meanwhile the other trucks drove over and parked.

"This calls for a drink I think," the American said. "Let's sit down."

"Excellent. Sergeant post a couple of sentries and get something to eat. I'll check on you later."

Drinks were passed around, cigarettes were lit, there was a comforting smell of cooking in the air. They talked. Isabel sat close to Cecil and held his hand tightly, looking at him now and then, as if to see if he was still there. Cecil was in Heaven.

"So what happened to your trip to Darfur?" he asked.

"We couldn't go. There was some sort of trouble with some of the tribes and someone suggested we come here, instead. There's lots for the customers to see here. We go to Suakin tomorrow and then to Port Sudan, where we take a boat to Brindisi and then on the Rex to New York."

"My God, what a journey. So this is it. I won't see you again?"

"Oh I hope so. I'll steal into your tent after lights out and have my way with you."

"Darling, I shiver with delight!"

"And I hope, one day you will come to America, and, who knows?"

Cecil thought about this last comment and pondered as he lay on his truckle bed. 'Fat chance.' The idea of being able to visit her in America was as unlikely as a trip to the moon. His career was here, and at some time in the near future, Palestine. Oddly enough though, when he thought of America as a destination, he thought of Susan, in Canada. The memories began to percolate: 'Dear Susan.' It all seemed so long ago now, so ethereal, like a dream.

A faint scuffling sound outside his tent made him sit up. He reached for his gun. The flap was pulled aside. It was Isabel. She came in and sat on the bed which creaked loudly.

"Oh dear, will we wake the others up?" she giggled.

"I don't care if we do," said Cecil. All thoughts about the future vanished.

"Come here you darling."

She slipped off her gown and slipped naked into his arms. It's likely that they woke up the whole surrounding desert for miles, but no one disturbed them.

Morning came too soon of course. Cecil raised himself onto one elbow and looked at Isabel, still sleeping. 'I could love this girl.' She was lovely, had humour, was as straight as an arrow, honest, forthright and kind. 'But America?' His heart dropped. 'It can't be done.'

A commotion outside attracted his attention. He pulled his trousers and boots on, after checking for scorpions, and pulled the tent flap back. An armoured car complete with machine gun, stood outside looking menacing. The constables were looking at it with rifles pointed. Manners was appearing from his tent, revolver in hand.

"What's going on?"

"It's an Itie!" shouted Cecil noting the insignia on the turret. At that moment a door in the side opened and a little white handkerchief tied to a stick was poked out.

"No one shoot," shouted Manners. "Hold your fire."

The door opened wider, and with stick raised high, out stepped an Italian army officer bearded and mustachioed. He turned to Manners and clicked his heels saluting.

"Capitano d'Abruzzi. Tre Regimenti di Bersaglieri. I ask your help signor Colonello. My men and I..." he turned to the car and beckoned quickly. Two soldiers stepped out with rueful expressions on their faces... "have been in action against the barbarous savages here who have killed the rest of my command. We are all that remains of my company. I fear that the enemy are on our heels as well. Only the car saved our lives, being faster than they could run. Though," he said, "not that much faster. They will be upon us any moment."

"Right," said Manners returning the salute. "Abdullah, strike camp. Two men on to that ridge. Signal if there's anything in sight. Everyone..." he turned to the Americans... "pack up and get in your car. There's not a moment to lose. Paynter, Thompson, get ready to move, Let's go. You too Isabel," he said sternly.

She giggled and ran to her tent. "See you later darling."

The next few minutes were barely controlled chaos. Finally, everyone was ready to move. Manners stood on the bonnet of the car and waved to the sentries on the hill.

"Retire lads. To me, to me." The constables came at a loping run, rifles at the trail.

"Any sign of anyone?"

"Yessir. Dust clouds not far. Be here soon."

"Okay. Off we go then. You chaps lead. Then the Yanks, then us. You, *capitano*, bring up the rear."

"Yes, my *colonello*. We serve with the Ingleezis. That is good."

The whole column prepared to move off. Cecil, looking back, saw a group of Beja warriors on camel. The group got bigger, until the whole slope was black with tribesmen waving spears and swords.

A puff of smoke appeared and Cecil heard the rattle of gunfire. Then the sound of wasps buzzing passed over his head.

"Christ chaps. They're not bad shots. Heads down."

Worse was to come. Some of the natives had got closer and were within spear throwing range. There was the most enormous whooshing sound and a great black coffin-headed spear thudded into the ground at his feet.

"Christ almighty! Open up with the Maxim!" he yelled at the Italian in the turret of the car. The soldier nodded excitedly and disappeared inside. In seconds the machine gun went into action, rat-at-tat-tat. The rounds went sparking off the rocks, ricochetting into the blue. Some black figures fell. Cecil quickly made for his car. Manners was already at the wheel, engine roaring. They moved slowly at first, then as tyres got traction, faster and faster. Now they were rocketing down the slope leading to the open desert.

Cecil swung around in the seat. The car containing the Americans and Isabel was running just in front, being driven by one of the Sudanese constables. Isabel waved. She was laughing and yelled something Cecil couldn't hear. But she seemed to be enjoying herself. 'What a girl' Cecil thought.

He looked around as he reloaded his revolver. Everyone seemed to be there, all going as fast as the terrain allowed. The Italian armoured car was bringing up the rear, its gun still chattering. The tribesmen were keeping a respectful distance from it. The dust trailing behind their little convoy was now starting to obscure them.

This continued for about an hour, when Manners, blowing the car horn, signaled to the others to halt. An impromptu meeting took place. Manners gave his opinion: that though they had probably lost the enemy, they should keep going as far as possible before night fell.

"Let's see. Where are we exactly Navigator?" He looked at Tony. "As if you'd know."

They all laughed.

Isabel, who looked stunning, flushed, and exited, said, "You Brits. So cool."

"You're pretty cool yourself," said Cecil.

"Oh, I thought it was marvellous. I don't know about my friends though," she looked at the elderly Americans.

"Oh we're okay. What a story to tell when we get back to Ohio."

"You chaps did well," Manners remarked to the Italians. "Thank God you had the machine gun. That did the trick."

"Thank you my Colonello," answered the Italian officer, beaming with pride and patting the bonnet of his car. "Maria, she good girl." The other two Italian soldiers nodded and grimaced, and rolled their eyes.

"Right. So let's have a look at the map. Abdullah, this

well here, Abu Hamed, any water d'you think?"

"Maybe sir."

"It has been a dry season and it's a bit off our track. Still the Italians look as though they might need extra water for their car." They both looked over at the steaming radiator. "Yes, we had better risk it. We should be safe from any more interference from the fuzzies."

"Yes sir. I think so sir."

"Right. Here's the plan." He turned to the others and explained the modus operandi.

After hours of hot dusty driving, the shimmering horizon, waving and undulating with false promises all about them, they finally reached the wells at Abu Hamed. Manners got out and stretched.

"Well, even if there is no water here, I think we should make camp. It's four now. By the time we get set up it'll start getting dark."

"Good idea sir." Cecil was relieved. He thought he'd go mad if they kept up much longer. He went around to all the others who were all yawning, and obviously ready for a break, and told them of Manners' decision. They were all as pleased as he was.

Cecil and Tony posted sentries. They would have a two hour watch each. Cecil drew the morning one, four to six. Later, they all sat around the fire, again sipping whiskey from enamel cups and puffing cigarettes. Cecil and the rest of his party had run out of their English brands and were now smoking American Lucky Strikes. They weren't half bad.

Abdullah banged the pans together to announce dinner. So they picked up and moved to the table, on which was placed a hurricane lamp and some tin plates. They sat expectantly. Abdullah spooned some grey porridge-like substance onto each plate and announced "Dhurra. Native corn. Good." Also, and like a conjurer producing a rabbit from a hat, some slices of meat that had been fried. "Desert Fox. You like."

"Abdullah! I don't know how you do it. You're marvellous," said Manners. In an aside to Cecil he said "More like desert dog I'd say, but don't say anything. It'll upset him."

"Actually it's quite good."

"Delicious," said Isabel tucking in. They all agreed and held up their mugs.

"To the chef. Abdullah. Hear, Hear."

Cecil looked over at the Italians. They were spooning in the food like starving men. God knows when they had last eaten.

"Everything alright D'Abruzzi?"

"Oh, yes sir. It is good to eat again. Salute!" he raised his mug of wine. Cecil thought, 'These Italians are alright.'

"Well, let's all be off to bed everyone." Manners stood up.

"Gee Homer," said the American lady. "This is like being back at camp when we were kids, only this is more fun."

"It sure is honey. I can't remember when we've had more excitement." They all laughed.

Manners continued. "Paynter. Don't forget, you've got

the morning watch. I'd get some sleep if I were you. He looked meaningfully at Isabel.

"Yes sir. I will. Of course." He looked appealingly at Isabel. She smiled.

"You're both right. A girl's got to get her beauty sleep after a day like that."

The night passed quietly. Cecil was glad to have a rest without interruption, even from Isabel. The last few days had exhausted all his resources. Replenishment was needed.

"Sir. Sir." A voice whispered in his ear.

"Yes, yes. What is it? It's four, sir. Your watch."

"Of course. Of course. Thank you Ali." He got up wearily and threw some water in his face from the basin. Outside he settled down, his back to a boulder. He gazed around and above. The sky was its usual magical sight. He held his breath for a moment trying to absorb the wonder of it all. It was as if all the stars were suspended in a drooping transparent sack, the nearest one so close that it would be easy to pick it up and place it on a rock nearby to light the camp.

He thought about everything he could to keep himself awake. Not easy. The couple of hours he'd slept hardly scratched the surface of his weariness. 'God. Wait until we get back to Khartoum, I'm going to sleep for a week. Christ! What the hell was that?' A scrabble of falling stones somewhere nearby startled him.

"Hello. Who's that?" he shouted, feeling somewhat stupid.

"Alright old boy. It's just me come to relieve you."

"Oh bless you Tony. I thought those two hours would never end, and then thought you were the whole bloody enemy. I was about to wet my pants."

"No, only me. It'll be dawn soon. Better get some shut eye."

"Thanks, I will. See you at breakfast."

"Right. Off you go."

As he fell onto his cot, Cecil was vaguely aware of a lightening in the eastern sky. Too tired to care, he drowned into darkness, to dream that he was home in green coolness and that Rowena was stroking his head.

Return To Khartoum...

The sound of an engine roaring woke him in the morning. He struggled out of deep sleep trying to make some sense of the noise. Sitting up and stretching, yawning and bleary, he finally managed to pull himself together enough to peer outside. It was the Italians with their armoured car. They were obviously having some trouble. Everyone else was sitting around the fire having breakfast.

Cecil hurried through his morning routine. 'God, it will be nice to return to some civilisation and creature comfort.' He thought wistfully of the lovely bathroom at his mess, with its wonderful facilities that he had taken so much for granted, and what he was having to go through now, the life-adventurous had its moments, to be sure. Its drawbacks were becoming onerous however.

"So what's up?" He strolled up to the breakfasting group. A chorus of morning greetings commenced.

"How did you sleep darling?" Isabel asked with concern.

"Pretty good dear," he replied.

"Actually, I slept well. Feel good. What's up with the Italians?"

"Oh, poor buggers, Can't start their machine. Apparently the corporal was Bugatti's chief mechanic before he signed up and even he can't get it going."

"Coffee?"

"Yes. Thanks Tony." He sat down next to Isabel. She gave him a kiss which made him blush. "Sorry darling," she laughed. "I missed you last night. Can't keep my hands off you now."

Manners spoke. "Alright. When you lovebirds have quite finished, better start packing up and be ready to squeeze them in with us," he motioned to where the Italians were. "They are not getting anywhere with that pile of junk."

"Right you are sir. Okay darling we should be in Khartoum tonight. I'll buy you dinner in the Grand Hotel."

"That's a date sweetheart," she laughed.

At that moment there came a shout from one of the constables posted on a nearby hill. Everyone stopped what they were doing and looked up. He came running, rifle at the trail.

"They come, they come, *Hadendoa*. Coming quickly."

"My god how could they have made it here so quickly?"

"Yes, they are sprightly blighters. Alright, drop everything. We don't have a moment to lose. Come on Georgio, or whatever your name is, mount up. Lets go. Dump anything that's not packed."

Engines started up all round, except for the armoured car that sat looking rather disconsolate. Manners looked around.

"All ready?"

The Italians were now squeezing in with Cecil and Manners. 'Oh, this is going to be great. All the way to Khartoum like this. Christ! Never mind. Here they come.'

Over the slope behind came a great galloping mob of natives on camels waving spears and rifles, yelling and screaming.

"Fire a few shots over their heads." With grinding gears and roaring straining engines, they all took off, a few shots crackling from the last vehicles containing the constables. Bucking and rolling, they all went hell-for-leather down the stony slope leading to the open desert, and safety.

"Well I think that's enough excitement for one day," remarked Manners. "You alright back there you chaps?"

The Italians, all three of them, were squeezed in the back.

"Si, si colonello. All ok here."

"Good. Let's see." He looked at his watch. "It's noon now. We should get to the Nile about four, then we'll be on the track to Khartoum. Should get there about six."

"Thank God for that," said Cecil.

"You'll be wanting to get back to Cairo to report I suppose?"

"Yes I should sir, I should, but I must say, I've rather enjoyed myself here."

"Well, we've been happy to have you. Come back any time.

It was just starting to get dark when they hit the road to Khartoum. They had stopped for a short rest which had put them behind, but now they were running on a smoother surfaced road and could start making better time.

By the time they got to the north end of the city it was seven p.m. and the night was quite black. Manners drove with his usual expertise, negotiating the crowded streets with great aplomb, finally reaching the main road that ran alongside the Blue Nile, passing the Grand Hotel with its gardens lit and dance music floating out of the brilliant mirrored rooms, then, passing the Great Governor General's Palace where Gordon had been killed so many years ago, but looking magical tonight, glowing in the floodlights, the statue of the great General himself in the garden mounted on his camel and shaking his riding crop at eternity.

Manners remarked, "We'll have a drink and dinner at the Grand soon."

"You bet," said Cecil.

"Well, here we are boys," laughed Manners as he wheeled into the courtyard of Police HQ. "The end of the road."

Everyone jumped out, stretching and yawning. They were all there: the Americans and the Italians looking about them with bewilderment, then the marvellous Sudani constables, grinning and happy to be home, and, closer to him, Manners, looking tired, but still cool, calm, and collected, Tony and the new officer, both looking a little distracted and weary, but smiling. What a journey they had had. What tales they would tell one day.

"Well, D'Abruzzi, it's time to say *arrivederci.*"

"Ah yes. Yes sir. It has been an honour to fight side by side with the Ingleezi."

"Yes. Quite. Quite. Well, look here. Will you and your men have dinner with us tonight? A sort of farewell meal. We should be delighted."

"*Grazi. Grazi.*"

"Come back with us to our mess. You can clean up and have a rest, alright?"

"*Perfecto. Admirablia!*"

Isabel and her friends were bundled into a taxi, which had appeared from nowhere. They were to go to the hotel where they would all meet later.

It was some two hours afterwards that they were being seated at a long table in the dining room. Their entry into and through the halls of the hotel had occasioned some excitement, as friends recognised each other. The Italians in their distinctive uniforms, now clean and pressed, and which included flat but dramatic helmets of a shiny black patent leather with a low crown, worn at an extreme angle over their right shoulder and which sprouted flamboyant black cock feathers, attracted especial attention. Everyone knew that one day they might be our enemies, but for tonight that was all forgotten. They were plied with drinks and their swarthy handsomeness caused many a flutter among the ladies.

When finally all the fuss died down, they were settled at their table and the laughter began, not to end until well past midnight, when sheer exhaustion forced them all to seek rest. The Italians swore undying allegiance to the King of England and all to each other.

Cecil and Isabel found a moment together in the garden

as they were all leaving. It was a difficult tearful moment, as they both knew that it was unlikely they would ever meet again. The romantic beauty of the gardens, now bathed in moonlight didn't help. Isabel was leaving early the next day to take the train to Port Sudan, where a cargo liner waited to sail to Italy, where they would take ship for the U.S. Cecil had to attend meetings at HQ and then return to Cairo and whatever waited for him there. This was goodbye.

"Oh my darling," Isabel whispered, "I shall miss you so much. It was all so wonderful, all of it. The last few days like a dream. I will never forget you. Write when you can and perhaps you might find yourself in America." She kissed him, her lips salty and wet. "Oh dear, what a mess. I'm sorry."

"No, no. Here let me," he dabbed at her face clumsily with handkerchief. He could hardly speak. He sounded husky and gravelly.

"Look. One day, who knows, I might turn up on your doorstep. I will write. I promise."

"It was rather marvellous, wasn't it? And my sweet, so are you. Now I think they need you." The others were waiting where the taxis stood. "Go. Don't forget me."

"I won't, ever."

She turned and ran down to the others.

The next morning came, and so did the next. Then the days ran together in a blurred, sad, empty, and meaningless greyness. The nights were unspeakably grim. He couldn't get Isabel out of his mind. Work seemed pointless. Play consisted of getting drunk every night at the Grand Hotel men's bar.

Then trying to sleep, and hoping not to dream was awful. He felt hopeless and without joy.

BACK TO CAIRO...

At last he got his orders to proceed to Cairo. He was, in addition, to travel by the new Imperial Airways Flying Boat which began its journey in Capetown and finished in London.

He felt the weight of his depression lifting. He was young and resilient. The period of feeling sorry for himself was passing. The prospect of returning to Cairo was helpful in making his spirits rise, so that on the day he said goodbye to all his friends, who came to the jetty on the White Nile to see him off, he was feeling quite elated.

Everyone had come down to say goodbye. Manners, Tony, and, he was pleased to see, the Sudanese constables, who were very affected and looked sad. Abdullah, who he really liked and who always smelt of cinnamon, shook his hand warmly, and though his mouth was smiling, his eyes were weeping, the tears running down his beautiful cicatriced black face.

Cecil, last to board, turned to step into the motor launch that was waiting. The Airways officer gave orders to cast off and the engine started up with that distinctive sound of the marine engine. It burbled away, heading for the plane that was lying, rocking gently, in mid stream. Cecil stood in the stern and looked back. They were all waving. A faint cheer floated across the water. He felt close to tears. The motor boat came alongside the open door in the side of the giant aircraft. The men at the bow steadied the craft with boat hooks while lines were cast and caught. The boat came to a standstill.

"All aboard ladies and gentlemen."

The small group of passengers climbed onto the flight deck. Cecil was the last. He took one last look at the riverbank. They were still there.

Inside, the cabin was full. The seat he had was the last empty one. It was well back on the right hand side.

"Your seat sir." A white jacketed steward spoke.

"Thank you." He settled into what was, in effect, a wicker armchair, the sort one sees in gardens and verandahs. The difference here was this one was fixed to the floor, and there were seat belts to fasten.

In what seemed a very short time, the engines started up with a great bang, emitting clouds of smoke. The whole airplane shook and trembled, then seemed to calm down and began a lovely contented purring drone. Shouts and yelled orders came faintly from outside. Cecil, craning his neck, could just see Arabs in a dinghy unfastening ropes that had held the aircraft to a river buoy. The plane began to move.

First she glided south on the river, then turned and pointed towards the north, then stopped. The engines were revved up until they seemed about to explode, then a moment of calm stillness, then they were off, pounding the surface of the river. Cecil felt his back pushed into the seat. 'This is extraordinary!' The heavy river water lost its grip and they floated free. Then, a second or two later, crash! They hit the water with a thudding splashing thump, and then, free again, soaring, flying, climbing, the motors roaring with full power, strong and satisfying.

A feeling of excited contentment crept over Cecil as he took a last look at Khartoum, dun and brown in the morning sun, with the ribbons of the Blue and the White Niles coming together at their confluence to make the great waterway that would roll to Egypt and the Mediterranean Sea.

The steward approached with a menu.

"A drink before lunch sir?"

"Yes please. A gin sling I think."

"Yes sir. Of course sir."

'This is rather nice,' thought Cecil, as he gazed around the cabin and out of the porthole, then at the menu card in his hands. 'Hmm,' they must have a little galley. Hmm. Sole meuniere. This is alright.' He lit a cigarette, sighed, and leaned back in his seat.

"Your drink sir. Lunch will be ready soon."

"Oh thanks."

"Take your time."

"I might have another drink then."

"Right sir."

Cecil sipped. It was just right, iced, lemony, and refreshing. The glass was misty and cold. It was pleasantly cool in the cabin. At the altitude they were flying, the outside temperature would be temperate and much different than the heat at ground level. He wondered how high they were.

Looking down, he could see still some detail: the river which they were following, was distinct, as were boats sailing on it. Little villages appeared and vanished. Rocky hills were quite clear, though without shadow.

Lunch arrived with the other drink, which he polished off before tucking into a really nice fish which was served with peas and little new potatoes. He noticed, under a napkin on the tray, dessert, which was melon and ice cream. He smiled to himself thinking about where he had been a few weeks ago, down there. He glanced at the desert below and shivered.

Lunch over, trays cleared away, it was time for a snooze. He settled back in the chair and slept... .

"Excuse me sir."

"What. What. What is it?"

"Sorry to wake you sir, but Captain Grahame, our chief pilot, wondered if you would like to join him in the cockpit for our descent into Cairo."

"Good Lord! What time is it?"

"It's four p.m. sir."

"God! I've been sleeping for two hours. Yes I'd be delighted."

Grahame? Of course. They had met at the Sudan Club a few weeks ago when the pilot had a stopover.

"Yes, lead the way."

The steward turned and went forward to the bow. Cecil followed. The plane was quite steady, so he had no difficulty in negotiating the narrow aisle.

"Here we are sir." A heavy green curtain was pulled

across and Cecil walked onto the flight deck.

"Well how are you Paynter. Welcome. Thought you might like to have a look at what goes on up front. Take a seat." He motioned to an empty leather bucket seat next to him. "Second pilot usually sits there. He's having a nap. Say hello to Chalmers, our engineer, and Patterson, radio and navigating expert. That's right strap in. Make yourself comfortable. We're over Luxor now, and will soon go into our descent to land, in about..." he looked at his watch, "er, half an hour. Yes, about five p.m. Just in time for drinks."

"Well this is exceedingly kind of you. The drinks will be on me when we get down."

Cecil was transfixed by the whole scene. Here they were, hurtling through space at about 300 mph, altitude probably 5000 feet, sitting calmly in this tiny compartment full of instrument panels, levers, switches, and dials, with perhaps forty passengers sitting behind them. This modern machine with great throbbing engines on either side. Cecil glanced out of the windows at the oil-streaked monsters with their whirling propellers. They were about to land at one of the really ancient places on the earth, the land of the Pharaohs, the Sphinx, and the Pyramids. He shook his head. It was all too much.

He looked ahead. The sun was sinking over to their left as they flew north, and the whole landscape ahead and below was bathed in a salmon pink glow. As they got lower, small villages began to appear, with roads, and little ant-like people moving about. This is all so strange, but there was more to come. The pilot flicked a few switches and began to throttle back the engines.

"We are going to begin the descent now I'll be a bit busy. Just relax and enjoy the view."

At this time of late day, the shadows were strong and long. Even the tiniest building was casting an enormous black shadow, making the whole scene even more dramatic. Now lights began to flicker below. They appeared to twinkle, and, as it got darker, it felt, looking up at the stars, as though the world was upside down. Cecil held his breath.

"Alright. Here we are." The pilot spoke as the plane banked gently and glided down a new path. Suddenly, the river appeared directly ahead. The city glittered around it. It was like they were dipping down into a an enormous cave of jewels.

"My God! This is fantastic!"

"Okay George. Give me flaps. Right. That's good." He handled the levers controlling power and the aircraft slowed. Now the surface of the river was clear below. The lights flashed by on both sides. A thud, and splash, and they were down. They bumped a few times, then moved slower and slower, until, with a flick, Grahame turned off the engines, and the great machine floated to a stop, rocking gently.

Cecil saw a motor boat approaching from the shore. After some conversation through the canopy between their engineer and the officer on the boat, docking instructions, by the sound of it, the boat crew made fast some towing wires and moved towards the shore towing them towards a jetty that stuck out into the river. They came alongside and were attached to the dock.

"Well, thanks for the ride Grahame. See you in the bar at the Continental."

"Right you are. Look forward to it."

"Around seven?"

"Perfect. See you then."

Cecil went back to the cabin where everyone was getting ready to disembark. He found his seat, and got ready to leave. As Cecil got nearer to the door he could feel the heat of the air outside. The sun was just about to disappear, so the evening cool hadn't begun, and as he stepped out onto the floating dock he felt the full force of the temperature. He looked about for a taxi or a carriage. A dilapidated old Ford Model T drove up. Cecil put his bags in the back and got in. He gave the driver the name of the hotel, sat back, and looked out at where the flying boat floated. It looked rather fragile and vulnerable.

The hotel was reached and Cecil booked in. This was the first time he'd stayed at the Grand Continental. Some friends had told him about it. It was less expensive than Shepheard's, but still comfortable and smart. He was shown his room, which was large and airy. He tried the bed. Lovely. He was looking forward to an early night. His orders were that he was to report to HQ immediately on arrival, so he planned to be at the office early next morning. He bathed and changed into a fresh outfit and felt better. He looked at his watch. 'Six. Let's see... he was to meet the pilot at seven. Okay, let's go.'

There was a funny little lift that one could take instead of the stairs. It looked like an elaborate bird cage, all convoluted iron work with lavish scrolling and intricate metallic tracery. It was heavily gilded in gold and silver and black and looked positively Byzantine. The whole contraption was operated by a wizened little Arab who looked at least 100 years old and was wearing a uniform that hung on him in folds. He spoke excellent English however, and informed Cecil, appropos of nothing, that when he was a operating this elevator as a young man, Lord Kitchener had taken passage in this strange machine when *Sirdar*, or Commander in Chief, of the Anglo-Egyptian army when conducting the River Campaign against the Dervish army in the 1890s.

Cecil thought again of the oddity of the last couple of days, the timelessness of the country and the ultimate 20th century journey on the aeroplane. He gave the old man a generous tip.

As he walked across the main lobby his name was called out. He turned. It was the receptionist.

"There is a message for you sir." The receptionist hastened around the front desk and came over to hand Cecil a piece of paper. It was from Grahame, the pilot, excusing himself from their planned meeting on the grounds of exhaustion. In a way Cecil was pleased. He was tired and only wanted a drink, a light meal, and bed.

He walked out on to the verandah where they were serving dinner in the cool night air. The captain led him to a table that looked out onto a large and fragrant garden where frangipani, mimosa and convolvulus climbed and tumbled. Beyond the garden and behind some large bushy trees, the sounds and sights of busy Cairo street traffic could be heard and just seen. It was Eastern magic and Western progress again. Cecil wondered again at the strangeness of it all.

He had a dry martini, a salad, and a good steak with a baked potato. Later for dessert, caramel custard. Finally he sat back with a tiny cup of Turkish coffee and puffed on a Balkan Sobrani cigarette. He was tucked in and fast asleep by ten o-clock.

A New Posting...

He felt refreshed when he woke next day and blessed his decision for an early night. He showered, shaved, and got dressed, and was soon running down the stairs. No lift this morning. He had a quick and minimal breakfast: coffee and toast, then to the desk to check out, which proceeded with much expression of good will on both parts and promises of future accommodations. A taxi was called and he was whisked off to headquarters, which to his embarrassment turned out to be practically next door. He felt a tip was not called for and left in a cloud of mutual recriminations, rather spoiling his mood.

Inside, that same old smell. Police stations must smell the same all over the world. He opened the door of the office he shared with Peter Foster, who was sitting at his desk and looked up with a smile.

"Oh, nice to see you Cecil. It's been quiet while you've been away now. Perhaps we'll have some fun again."

"Hello old boy. Have you seen my brother?"

"Yes. He's around somewhere. How was the Sudan?"

"Oh, quite exciting. You should try it sometime. Have you had your coffee yet?"

"No. Chap's a bit late. Oh here he comes now."

"Jolly good. Is that the morning paper over there?"

"Yes. Want to read it?"

"Yes please. Thanks." Cecil sat back, sipped his coffee, and caught up on world news with The Egyptian Gazette. The date was December 15th 1935. He scanned the headlines. "This Hitler chap's a bit of a bore isn't he?" At that moment the door opened and his brother Nigel walked in.

"Oh, you're back. Good show. How was it?"

"Bloody marvellous. Fell in love, got chased and shot at by a bunch of Fuzzy Wuzzies and almost died in the desert. Yes all and all, a good trip I should say. How are you?"

"Good. I'm going on leave soon, so its timely that you came back now, otherwise we'd have been short-handed."

"Oh, lucky fellow. Well you were due for home leave a few months ago and you didn't take it. Went off on some swan into the desert to see your beloved Bedouins."

"Yes, you're right."

"But I'm expecting to go to Palestine soon. I was promised that by the old man."

"I didn't know that you'll be as keen as you were about that posting old boy. There's all sorts of trouble there now between the locals and all the Jews pouring in from Europe. This Hitler chap's making it bloody unpleasant for those poor sods."

"Oh, but I thought we had some sort of agreement about limited immigration?"

"We did, but they are coming in hordes anyway, regardless. The Arabs are up in arms about it all. It's a bloody mess."

"Well, all the more reason for me to go and try to help."

"Good luck. Shall we have dinner tonight"

"You bet. Let's."

The phone on Cecil's desk rang. He picked it up. "Hello?"

It was the chief. "Heard you were back. Your posting's come through. Ready to go to Haifa next week?"

"Yes sir."

"Good. Come and see me. I'll give you the details."

"Cecil ran up the stairs two at a time. This was what he wanted, and he was elated.

"Come in, come in," Ferguson's unmistakable voice called out. Cecil opened the door. "Ah, Paynter, my dear boy. Nice to see you. Sit down, sit down. Have a cigarette. Some coffee?"

"Oh thank you sir."

Ferguson had an odd and rather startling affliction in that he would sometimes suffer the equivalent of a stutter, which took the form of him pausing in speech, tightly screwing up his eyes, stiffening in his chair, then bursting into a shouted command, or just a quiet comment. In this case it was a roaring order.

"Suffragi! Gahwa!" With uncanny speed and in total silence, a little old man in the garb of a servant appeared with the brass, glass, and copper utensils requisite for a good cup of coffee.

"Ah, thank you Ibrahim. He's been with me since I came out in 1919. Wonderful old chap. Old as the hills. Remembers

Gordon. Now then, where are those orders? Had 'em here just now. Ah. Here we are." He shuffled through some papers, looked at them for a second or two, and looked up at Cecil. His expression was one of candid concern.

"Now, you know this is not going to be any picnic. The balloon's going to go up good and proper one of these days soon. The Zionists are really determined they are going to have their way with full emigration, even if it means bloodshed. The Grand Mufti and the Arabs conversely, are dead set against them, and we are in between trying to sort things out. You are going there because we think your fluency with some of the lingo they speak among the Bedou could be useful in certain hush hush ways."

Cecil felt a little unease.

"You mean I'm going to be a spy sir?

"No, no. I wouldn't put it that way. More like intense liaison between sides. You'll be seconded to the Palestine Police boys, wear their kit, all that sort of stuff. You'll be stationed in Haifa, but will go all over. This is an important job for you Paynter. You will do your best to ameliorate the feelings between local desert Arabs and the Jewish settlers in their areas. You know the form. Lawrence made promises to the Arab for their help against the Turks. Promises that we have tried to keep, and of course we made promises to the Jews when Mr. Balfour said that His Majesty's Government looked with favour on the establishment of a Jewish homeland in Palestine. But rightly or wrongly, the government has had to make changes for a variety of reasons. French demands for

Syria and excessive Jewish demands for larger areas of settlement. We thought we could keep them all happy, but we were not prepared for Mr. Hitler and his nastiness with these poor people. Forced to come in droves instead of dribbles. Alright?"

"Yes sir. I will do my best."

"Yes, I know you will. Good luck my boy. Write to me directly if anything comes up that you're uncomfortable with."

"Thank you sir. That's reassuring."

"Good, good. Off you go. It's all rather like a cricket match, what? Going in to bat against the fast bowling."

Cecil couldn't think of a reply to this and decided to remain silent. He went out of the office and down the stairs less happily than when he had gone the other way. 'Still,' he thought, 'it's a big job and when it's over I'll go home on leave. Who knows what may happen in the weeks and months ahead.' He would have reason to remember that specific thought with some degree of irony.

Nigel and Peter were waiting for him.

Okay, let's go and have some lunch."

"Who's paying?"

"I suppose I should," said Cecil. "After all I'm the one who's going off again."

"Good show. Where shall we go?"

"Groppis, I say."

"That's a bit steep. Oh, alright."

"My car's outside."

They went chattering down the steps to where a canary

yellow Riley was parked.

"It's a bit of a squeeze. It's really a two-seater, but we'll manage." They all climbed in somehow and Peter pressed the starter. The engine clamoured into a rattling shaking roar.

"Christ Peter. What's this got under the bonnet?"

The rest of the week passed uneventfully, except that every night was party-night all in honour of his imminent departure. The posting would be for a year Cecil discovered. The way everyone was behaving, one would think he was going forever. His brother had been up there for a while and had met a dishy American girl. He remembered Nigel mentioning how smitten he was. He would look her up. She had apparently had some dealings with Colonel Lawrence, ran a hospital or something.

The day of departure finally arrived and a rather limp and very hung over Cecil was driven to the station by Peter, who was equally fragile and whimpering about getting back to bed. Cecil thought, 'hope nobody breaks the law any where near us. We'd be totally useless.'

The station reached, they were overwhelmed by offers of help to carry baggage. That was sorted out and they followed the bearer of the bags out onto the platform, where the night express for Haifa was waiting. A compartment was found, goodbyes said, Peter left, and Cecil fell back against the seat and looked around.

The compartment was fairly comfortable, sparse, but quite spacious. The fact that he had it to himself was a fluke of the highest order. He looked out of the window. The platform was empty of potential passengers. A few station staff were standing about. He saw the guard lifting a whistle to his lips and unfurling a green flag. He looked at his watch. 'Bloody marvellous.' It was leaving time. The whistle blew, the engine ahead answered with a hoot, and the train began to move. Cecil sat back and watched the streets of Cairo pass. At every intersection there were groups of children playing who stopped and waved at the train. Cecil waved back, and suddenly had a feeling of deep melancholy.

TRIP TO PALESTINE...

He must have gone into a deep sleep, as the next thing he was conscious of, was being spoken to. He woke and saw the inspector and assistant hovering over him with hands out for tickets. He fumbled around in his kit bag and found them. They were clipped and with many *salaams* the officials left. He felt the usual grumpy sleepiness one does after an afternoon nap that went on too long.

He had lately learned the life-saving trick of power naps instead of long siestas, and he always felt refreshed and alert after them. This had been, he checked his watch, two hours. A long one. He washed his face and hands in the tiny basin, and brushed his hair, and felt better. It was about four o'clock, time for tea. He pressed the bell for the steward.

Tea arrived, a nice big pot, and on the tray with the milk and sugar, cup and saucer, was a little plate of ginger biscuits, his favourite. Pouring the tea he remembered his nanny admonishing him, 'milk first Master Cecil, remember.' Why on earth did he think of that? He felt again that strange feeling of sadness that he had yesterday. Odd. He sipped the tea and crunched a biscuit, crisp and thin and gingery.

After tea he lit a cigarette and relaxed, looking out the window. They were running through the green irrigated part of lower Egypt between the capital and Port Said where the Suez Canal began. He was looking at the great river's gift to Egypt, the waters that had begun from a thunderstorm over the mountains of Abyssinia for the Blue Nile or from rains over Lake Victoria in Central Africa for the White Nile, which then had flowed sluggishly through the Sudd, the great papyrus swamp of the Southern Sudan.

The train was now clacking over a complex of points, obviously a junction. He looked at his map. 'Ah yes. This is where the line divides. We go north, the other ones go south and south west, one to the other end of the canal at Kantara, and the other to Luxor and southern Egypt.'

It would not be long before they get to Port Said. In fact at that moment the line turned to the north and the canal was reached. The train crossed it at a bridge. A cruiser of the Royal Navy waited to proceed. She looked very sea-worn, stained and grimy, some bits of red lead paint flecked her bow. Some sailors working on the forward deck waved and gave a cheer. 'Wonder where she's going?' thought Cecil as he waved back.

The train was now running due north and the suburbs of Port Said began to slip past. 'Funny,' he thought, 'this was where I came ashore so long ago.' They were in fact rattling along with the canal. On their left several ships were moored alongside docks. Out in mid stream, a big oil tanker, standing high in the water, obviously empty, steamed to the south, on her way back to the gulf for more fuel for thirsty Europe.

The shadowed platforms of the station now came into view, crowded with passengers-to-be, hawkers of every kind of merchandise, carts of baggage, vendors of food and drink, magazines and tobacco. With a grinding clanking crash the train stopped. Except for the whirring compartment fan and distant shouting, whistling, and slamming of doors, comparative quiet ensued. The end of the first stage of the journey had arrived.

Cecil opened the door and climbed down to the platform for a stretch and a look round. He strolled over to a news agent and bought some magazines and a newspaper, then to a man selling lemonade, a glass of which he sipped on the way back to the train. The drink was cool and refreshing.

Getting back to his compartment he found he had some new companions: two young men in the uniform of the Palestine Police.

"Hello."

They both sprang to attention, saluting, In their haste one of them almost knocked off his headgear, which was an Astrakhan Russian Cossack-style cap. At first Cecil wondered at their attitude then realised that he was the senior officer here. These two were just second lieutenants. He was now a *Bimbashi*, or Major.

"Oh do carry on. No fuss for me. I'm being seconded to your lot. Perhaps you could be of help to me. You know, what's the form and so forth."

"Oh yes sir. We certainly can. Anything you need. Of course, of course."

"Right. Well, first things first. Let's have a drink."

"Oh, good show sir, we have some gin, and ice too.

"Well done lads. I have some Angostura bitters. Terrific! pink gins with ice. What luxury." Cecil had invested in a small wicker picnic basket in which he kept the necessities of life: a flask of scotch, a small bottle of brandy, little strong glass tumblers, an opener, a corkscrew, some slabs of chocolate, and the tiny bottle of bitters that turned gin a transparent pink and was the favourite drink of the Royal Navy's wardrooms everywhere.

"Cigarette?" He passed around a package of Gold Flakes. They both took one and lit up.

"Cheers! Up the Navy! Thank God we've got an army!" they chuckled at the old toast and downed their drinks. Cecil poured fresh ones.

"So, what's it like up there?"

"Oh, alright. It's quiet most of the time. Now and again someone chucks a bomb at you. One never knows when it's going to happen. Illegals arrive almost every week now. The Navy tries to control things, but can't patrol the whole coast. Then the Arabs start throwing their weight around. Our poor chaps who have been issued sticks and a shield made of wicker to keep the stones off, are not very successful I'm afraid."

"Why aren't they armed ?"

"Oh the powers that be think in terms of the unarmed London Bobby. This isn't Piccadilly unfortunately."

"We don't want to hurt anybody either," the other officer put in.

"No. Quite, quite. By the way I'm Cecil Paynter."

"Oh, how d'you do. I'm Alan Davies and this is

Lieutenant John Driscoll."

"Oh, Welsh and Irish I presume."

"Right. In fact we only got here from the troubles over there six months ago. This is a piece of cake compared to Ireland and the bloody Sinn Fein. They are really tough and completely without mercy. A lot of local feuds settled under cover of patriotic zeal. Nasty business. Then our government brought in a bunch of thugs, ex-soldiers from the war, no jobs, you know, a few criminals, rotten lot. Anyhow they put them in a light khaki uniform with black leather equipment. Got called The Black and Tans of course. Boy oh boy, they out-did the rebels in brutality. Very unpleasant crowd, So we'd rather be here. So far, anyway."

Cecil nodded.

"Frankly, I think we've made too many promises to too many people, but what could we do? All these loads were heaped on us by the big boys at Versailles."

"Except for Ireland," put in Alan.

"Yes, right. But we had to think about the Ulster Protestants in the North. They would start a civil war if we abandoned them to the South. I just do not think we could have done anything else."

Cecil glanced out of the window. It was beginning to darken out over the desert. They would be coming into the Sinai soon, he estimated, so by morning they would be crossing the border into Palestine.

"Let's go and see what's for dinner, shall we?"

The food available, in what passed for a dining car, an

antique carriage once belonging to the old Hejaz Railway and run by the Turks during the war, was limited to sandwiches and soup, but hungry as they were, they tucked in with relish. Odd to think that this coach might once have been the target of Lawrence and his Arabs.

"Yes sir. The food's not bad."

"No, actually quite good. At least the bread's not stale."

Cecil wiped some crumbs from his mouth.

"Well, it's me for heads down. We should be well over the border by morning. Let's hope we have a quiet night."

"The Arabs have been a bit troublesome on this stretch of line I understand. The odd explosive on the track."

"Yes. It's not been too bad lately. At one time they ran a truck in front of the engine just in case."

"Is that so?" Cecil looked out of the open window, and screwing up his eyes against sparks and cinders flying through the air, squinted ahead. The locomotive was only a couple of coaches in front of them, big and black with a great searchlight shining ahead.

"Ouch!" A hot bit of grit stung his cheek. 'Well enough of that.' He withdrew his head from the night air.

"I'm for shut eye. Ready chaps?"

"Yes, lets go."

They made themselves as comfortable as they could. Cecil and the senior of the two subalterns lay full length on the two benches, and the junior lay on his bedroll on the floor. The train swayed and clanked through the night with an occasional hoot from the engine. They slept.

The morning came all too soon. Cecil opened one eye and looked blearily at his watch. Seven. The sun was already bright. Although they had wooden-slatted shutters on the windows, the gleams of light shone through the gaps, bathing the cabin in a pale lemon yellow wash.

"Wake up chaps."

Two groans answered him, but Davies, the older one rolled over and said, "What's the time?"

"Sevenish. Thought I'd see if there's any coffee to be had.""

"Good idea sir."

"Oh do stop calling me sir. The name's Cecil."

"Oh good show. I'll join you. Get up you lazy bugger." He shook his companion.

"I'm awake, I'm awake."

"Okay. Were going to look for *gahwa*. Want some?"

"You bet."

They both went rolling down the corridor trying to balance against the swaying of the train.

At that precise moment there was the most enormous explosion of sound and light, together with violent movement, first one way then another. They were both thrown to the floor and rolled about helplessly as the carriage tipped one way, then another. The noise and movement ended as suddenly as it had begun, and now there was just the sound of whistling steam escaping in a high pitched screech.

Cecil dragged himself to his feet.

"What the hell was that?"

"A mine on the line, I wouldn't be surprised," said Davies. "We've been derailed."

"Better get back to the cabin and get our revolvers. One never knows. They might be out there waiting to jump us."

They staggered back and managed to open the jammed sliding door, Driscoll was crouching under the window peering out, pistol cocked.

"God, glad you re back. I think it's an ambush."

Cecil extricated his Sam Brown and holster from his bag and pulled the revolver out, checked it for ammo – it was loaded – flicked off the safety, and cautiously looked out of the window. He could see nothing, just sand dunes and miles of empty desert. Not a sight of life.

"No one out there old boy. I think its just a bomb on the line."

"Okay."

"Better see who's in charge of this train and what we're going to do about this mess."

Smoke was pouring past the window from the stricken locomotive. Some of it came into the train causing them to choke and cough.

'The hell with it. I'm going outside.' Cecil leaped to the ground just a few feet below and crouched, looking about. Nothing stirred.

"Come on chaps. Let's see what's up front."

The others dropped down beside him. Then, looking alertly around as they went, they ran forward to the engine. It was still upright on its wheels but its front end was firmly in the sand. The driver and fireman were crouching down, their eyes wide with fear. Cecil spoke to them in Arabic and told them to stay where they were and that all was well. They then relaxed and smiled weakly. One, the driver, remarked that this reminded him of the days he drove for the Turks and had been attacked by the great El Orrance, meaning T.E. Lawrence of course. They pronounced the name in their colloquial tongue.

At this point in the proceedings, some passengers had climbed down from the tilting first coach, and were standing around looking lost and uneasy.

"It's alright," Davies yelled. "Help will surely come soon," he said, looking at Cecil.

Now, from the second coach, which was still perched on the tracks, came another group of British officers, quite senior ones by the look of them. Cecil walked up and saluted. The older officer returned the salute. He was a full general. Cecil introduced himself.

"How do you do," said the general. "What are you?"

Cecil explained.

"Well what do you think we should do?"

Cecil's good luck came to his aid again, for he had no idea what to do, and the expression on the general's fierce red face was terrifying to see. Cecil began to blurt some nonsense when a shout from Driscoll made him look round.

"Here comes the bloody cavalry," laughed Davies, as a couple of old Rolls Royce armoured cars came rumbling over the horizon.

'Saved by the bell', thought Cecil.

The general looked mollified.

"Knew they were out there patrolling sir. Just a matter of time."

"Hrrumph," grunted the general, looking at him keenly.

"Well, what's your name?"

Cecil told him.

"I'll remember you," the General said, looking at him wryly.

The cars were up with them now. A young man in a cherry red beret jumped out of the turret and came to attention.

"Jones sir. 11th Hussars."

"Ah, yes. Capital. What's the form?"

"We have wireless contact with HQ sir. There will be transport here presently to take you to Gaza where another train will be laid on. This happens now and then. We have the form down pretty well now."

"Right. Well let's get out of this heat and see if we can get some food and drink in the coach that's still on its legs."

They all trotted after him, that is, all except the armoured car people and Cecil, who spoke to the officer of the 11th Hussars.

"They call you "the cherry pickers" don't they?"

"Yes. It's because of the colour of our trousers and caps."

"Yes, I knew that. A friend's writing about the oddities of the British Army and you get a mention."

"Oh, interesting."

"You know the one about the 17th//21st Lancers? Didn't have a battle honour until Omdurman. They said their motto should be 'Thou shall not kill.' " They both chuckled.

"So, tell me about these cars. Are they the Duke of Westminster's old machines?"

"Yes. Came out in 1916. Used all through the desert campaign. It was said they never changed the oil."

"God! Magnificent!"

"Rather. Well here comes the transport."

Howling over the sands came two large lorries. They drove up in great style and stopped in a cloud of sand and diesel fumes, a couple of grinning Tommies in the front seat of both vehicles.

" 'Ere we are again. Where's our cargo sir?"

"You be polite. One of them's a general."

"Blimey! Better watch my manners."

"Yes, you better had." The lieutenant smiled.

After some initial fuss about baggage, they all climbed aboard the trucks and made themselves as comfortable as possible and were soon on their way.

As they climbed the first sloping sand hill, Cecil saw what he presumed was the repair train, an engine and two trucks coming down the line. 'They are pretty efficient here,' he thought.

Several very uncomfortable hours later they came to a metalled road and swung north, the glimmering Mediterranean Sea, its horizon seemingly higher than they were, was on their left. The fresh breeze blew gently and everyone began to smile.

"Shan't be long now," said one of the soldiers.

Gaza, though uninspiring in appearance, being just a few dun coloured buildings sprawling around a central market place with a Mosque and attendant minaret, looked like Heaven to the travellers. There was a small hotel which boasted a communal bath house, where they washed up, then they were fed in a shady courtyard at a long wooden table. Utensils and crockery were minimal, and had seen better days, but the food was wonderful. Arabic style: lots of rice with fish and chicken, home-made bread crusty and fragrant, and fresh goat's milk to drink. Then some gigantic watermelons, some figs, and apricots for dessert, with hot coffee to follow. They wolfed it all down then sat back and lit pipes and cigarettes.

"Now this is more like it," said the general puffing on a cigar.

They sat and chatted for a while, though the general did most of the talking. His name was Arlington and he was out from England on a fact-finding tour of the area. Basically, he was to advise on whether more troops were needed to keep the peace, and to listen to commanders on the ground regarding tactics and the best way to handle things. Evacuation was not an option. We had made promises to both sides and, of course, there was the oil. A pipeline was just being completed from Mosul to Haifa on the coast. Both British and American interests were involved, and, in fact, the line and terminus were owned and operated by an American company, the Iraq Petroleum Company.

Cecil glanced at his watch. It was late afternoon. He was tired. He thought, 'I'd like a drink and bed. Wonder how long this will go on?' His hopes were about to be vouchsafed him. A soldier came out to the courtyard and said something to one of the general's ADCs, who smiled and said, "They have made some rooms available in the hotel I'm sure you gentlemen will want an early night, so I suggest we go now and settle ourselves in. In addition I'm informed a train will be laid on for us first thing in the morning." He looked at a paper the soldier had given him. "Six a.m. alright?"

There was a general sigh of relief and everyone got up and started to leave, Cecil, Davies, and Driscoll staying together. They strolled down the palm-tree-lined street in the gathering dusk, the afterglow in the western sky a pearly aquamarine. Cecil felt very relaxed and a little smug.

The night passed in tranquility. A gentle breeze floated through the half-open shuttered window causing the sheer drapes to stir. The scent of mimosa came with it. The sheets were cool and smooth, the pillows soft but firm. Cecil turned over feeling utter comfort, and went to sleep.

New Chums...

Next day they all met in the lobby. Davies said, "Good oh! The British Army is paying the bill."

"Oh, well done," said Cecil.

"Any coffee?"

"Yes." Someone passed him a cup.

"Well good morning gentlemen. I've had my coffee. They will give us breakfast on the train I understand. Apparently the station is just a short walk, so if we're all ready. Lets go." They all trooped out, looking, Cecil thought, a bit like a school crocodile.

The station was reached. The train consisted of an engine, two coaches, and a truck with a Vickers machine gun heavily sandbagged in front.

They got aboard, and in no time, with a haughty hoot from the loco, they were off.

The outlying landscape, though still quite arid-looking, seemed somehow less like a desert, more like a gravelly plain, more like the Sudan, Cecil thought. Looking ahead he thought he could see a darker horizon, darker, and, could it be? Greener?

"I say chaps, look ahead. What do you see?"

"Looks like trees," said Driscoll.

"Yes, trees. I think we're coming up to the famous orange groves of Palestine," said Cecil.

The trees got closer and it was clear that there was some order about them. This was no natural growth. Then they were into them, as far as the eye could see, row upon row of small bushy orange trees, all with narrow irrigation ditches running between them. Small figures were dotted about working with tractors and ladders, tending the crops. It was marvellous. One moment sand and stone, savage, brutal, and unforgiving, the next, this: this paradise of green growth, cultivated and fertile. This was the work of the immigrants from other lands. They had made all this through sheer hard work and determination.

"You have to hand it to the Jews," said Davies.

"Indeed you do," replied Cecil. "This is quite fantastic."

As they kept going through this changed land, they began to see signs of habitation: small buildings grouped together with barbed wire fences. They noticed too, that some of the closer figures carried arms.

"I understand they are constantly under attack," said Driscoll.

"Yes, I believe they are," answered Cecil. "That's going to be my main job, trying to help stop the fighting between them and the Bedou."

"Good luck old man," said Davies dryly.

Cecil said, "Yes, and now I'm beginning to wonder about it all. I'd like to think I'm neutral in this fight, but I have in my heart liked and felt sorry for the Arabs up to now. Now seeing all this I don't know. This is going to be very difficult indeed."

They continued passing mile after mile of cultivated land, not all oranges, but, as well, what looked like barley. And perhaps fields of what might have been lettuce. There seemed to be all sorts of crops being grown and it all looked so unlike anything else he had seen since coming out East. 'Remarkable!' He pulled out his map case and started making notes of his observations.

"I say, Paynter." It was Davies.

"What is it old boy?"

"I presume you'll be reporting to our HQ when you get to Haifa."

"Yes, that's right. Why?"

"Well, we can toddle along with you. That's where we have to check in."

"Great. When do we get there?"

Davies looked at his watch. "About sixish I would say."

"Oh, just in time for drinks. Good show. I think I'll get a bit of rest. Let me know if anything happens.

"Wake up old chap." It was Davies shaking him. "We are coming in to Haifa."

Cecil dragged himself out of a deep sleep. "Oh are we here?"

"Yes. We're running through the outskirts now."

Cecil looked out through the window. On the right he could see the massif of what he assumed was Mount Carmel. The left-hand-side window framed a view of the sea. It was early evening and ships anchored off shore had their riding lights on. A cool breeze came through the open window. Cecil could smell oil. They must be near the terminus of the pipe line. The train's speed slackened and the whole long and eventful journey began to come to an end. He had the oddest feeling of completion, as though an important end to a chapter in his life had happened. No, it wasn't quite that. It was as though one were about to begin another one. A satisfying combination of both perhaps. Whatever it was, he felt elated, serene, and entirely happy.

The usual procedures were followed after suitable and cordial goodbyes to the general and his staff. Cecil and his new friends left the train and walked down the platform to the exit gates. The station was crowded with civilians, both Arab and European. Everyone seemed relaxed and normal. There was no apparent tension. A few soldiers strolled about. Here and there the odd armed policeman in the distinctive Astrakhan headgear of the Palestine Police Force. They walked out into the bustling street outside.

Davies said "If you don't mind a short walk, it's not far to the hotel we always use. It's quite nice."

"No. That's fine. It's good to stretch."

"Rather." said Driscoll. "Fresh air, what?"

The pavement was jammed with people, both adults and children. There was activity everywhere: what looked like families all promenading together in the pleasant evening air, looking in shop windows, smiling, laughing, talking. Little sidewalk cafes were everywhere, tables packed. Arabs were sipping coffee and smoking the hookah, the water pipe apparatus so common in the middle East. There was the sound of tinkling music, with someone singing in Arabic, the wailing voice sad and melancholy. Then, there was a restaurant with mostly Europeans drinking and eating, western music being played on a piano. 'Gershwin.' Cecil thought, 'Nice.' It all looked so normal and ordinary. 'Where's all the fuss and trouble,' he wondered. 'There didn't seem to be anything to worry about here.

There was an element though, that seemed not to belong here. This was the occasional group of what had to be Bedouins from the desert. Not many, but when you saw them, they were impressive, tall, lean, fiercely angry-looking. 'Oh, God!' thought Cecil. 'These are the ones I have to deal with.'

"Here we are lads. Not the best hotel in town. but clean and comfortable."

"Wonderful," said Cecil, looking up at the building, which in large neon lights pronounced itself "The Ritz." "Well it's got a good name anyway," laughed Cecil.

Checking in was quick and painless. After a refreshing bath and change they all met for dinner. The old hotel had seen better days, but the food was good, and the service pleasantly old-fashioned. The *maitre d'* was an old Frenchman who chatted with them for a while. He had come here from Syria, which the French were running, and he had married an Italian lady, who stayed in the background. She was obviously the power behind the throne, and probably ran the whole business. They had bought the place right after the end of the war and had settled down quite happily.

Dinner over, they said their goodnights and climbed wearily to bed.

Cecil's room was at the front of the building, so at first it was difficult to get to sleep. The sounds from the streets below were disturbing, as was a flashing neon light that flickered and sparked just outside his window. Finally the city settled down and began to go to sleep. Cecil floated away into oblivion with it.

REPORTING IN...

The next day dawned bright and hot. They met for breakfast and checked out. The Italian lady wished them *arrivederci* and out they went. A taxi was procured and drove them to police headquarters. It was the typical British style of architecture for these kind of buildings, unimposing, uncomplicated, no nonsense. The blue Palestine Police Flag billowed alongside the Union Jack. A flight of steps led up to the large doors. It could be Cairo, Khartoum, or any one of a hundred places in the countries that Britain controlled.

Through the doors, saluting as they went, constables running to and fro on their various duties, they walked briskly down a long passage. Wood and glass, just like Khartoum. The similarity was uncanny.

Davies, who was leading, stopped at a door marked Commandant, and knocked. They heard a voice bidding them enter. They went in, and coming to attention, saluted the figure behind the desk.

This was, Cecil discovered on introduction, the heavily decorated and extremely proficient commander of the Haifa area, whose name was Murdoch. He was also very popular, being of an amiable disposition and sociable in the extreme. He passed round a packet of cigarettes and clapped his hands ordering coffee when the *suffragi* came in.

"Well, I hear you chaps had a bit of a rough trip coming here. Tell me all about it."

They did. He looked at them in turn as they related their experiences.

"Well done! Now, Davies and Driscoll you two should report to your company commanders, so off you go. Paynter you stay for a sec so that we can see how you will fit in to the picture here. Now I understand your duties will be to assist in working with some of the tribes, keeping an eye on things, how they are reacting to the increase in immigration of Jews, and so on. Now we all know what their feelings will be. We have already seen what they have done, but we hope your branch will alleviate, in some way, their anger. You especially have been chosen because of your expertise in the languages they speak. You will work with Davies who has a line to some of the Sheiks. They seem to like and trust him. You will wear your own uniform with an armlet stating that you are a Supernumerary of the Palestine Police Force. Right. Go and find Davies. He will put you in the picture. But before you go, a word to the wise." He lit a cigarette and blew a smoke ring, Cecil watched it float up to the whirling ceiling fan and disappear.

"Now look here Paynter. I'll be candid with you. We all have a rotten job here. Nobody likes us and I don't particularly like them. I'd much rather be back home getting ready to retire to family and garden, but the hot potato has been handed to us to keep the peace as best we can. All we can hope is that some miracle will happen and they will learn how to get on with each other. Doubtful, but we must try to make it happen, otherwise there is going to be a bloody disaster. We are not without some responsibility for the state of affairs, making promises to both sides we can't keep."

"The promises to the Jews were through something called the Balfour Declaration. A chap called Weizmann was involved, along with some valuable technical help from the Jews for the British war effort. The reward for that was support from the British Government after the war for a Jewish homeland in Palestine."

"Anyway, along comes bloody Lawrence. He tells Feisal and the Arab tribes that they will get all sorts of territorial advantages. I mean kingdoms and gold beyond the dreams of avarice. Great chaps the Bedou, but do love their fun and games, which costs money. So here we are, not in a happy spot. Alright. I know you will do your best. Work closely with Davies. He's a good man."

Cecil found Davies who showed him a desk, the top of which was crowded with files, books, and papers held down from the fan-moving-air by paperweights in the form of those glass orbs that look as though they have something growing inside them.

"Look old boy. I don't know how much you know about the history of what's going on here, but you should read these books which will give you some idea of what brought us to the sorry state we are in now. Then there are some files on the families who pull some weight around here. Then there are some papers you should study about some of the rough boys on either side. Lot of dossiers there that will make your hair stand on end. You'll need lots of coffee to get through that lot. Let me know if any questions arise."

"Thanks Davies. I will." Cecil turned to the books first and started to read.

He learned about some of the origins of the conflict between Jew and Arab. He was surprised to discover, amongst other things, that in the late 1890s a Jewish writer and sometime Zionist activist, Theodor Herzl, had actively sought the support of the Kaiser of Germany, Wilhelm II, who was interested in the Middle East for political, economic, and military purposes, and because there was already a large German presence in Palestine in the form of religious groups of various orders. It seemed odd to Cecil to read about the Kaiser's tacit approval for a Jewish homeland to be established there, in light of what was happening in Germany to the Jewish people at this time. A further irony, he thought, was that the Zionist headquarters was in, of all places, Berlin.

Herzl, in any case, sought, and got an audience with the Kaiser, which took place in Jerusalem. The meeting took place, with the Kaiser being politely non-committal about the Zionists' ambitions.

Cecil learned something about the powerful Arab families, like the Husseinis and Khalidis who actively protested to the Ottoman government about the increasing purchase of land by the Jews. On the whole however, Jew and Arab got on well together. Many Arabs subscribed to the view that the Jews brought prosperity to their land and that they grew rich along with them. The Jews transformed what had been a wretched, arid, land of desert and swamp, into a relatively green, cultivated country with eucalyptus trees draining the soil where it was marshy, and orange groves where there was desert. Much of the work, for the time being, was done by the Arabs. Sadly this did not continue, as more and more of the work began to be undertaken by the Jews themselves. This became disagreeable to the Arabs, who then began to make things difficult.

Thus it was, that as more and more land was bought from the Arabs, and more and more immigrants arrived, and then disappeared into the country, even without passports, the Arab, and now the thoroughly alarmed Ottoman rulers, began to take steps to try to limit the influx of Jews. In the case of some of the locals, they resorted to violence. The Palestine offices run by the Jews throughout the world turned up the pressure to obtain extra funds to support their growing desire to enter the land, the Rothschilds being one of the leading funders of this movement.

This state of affairs continued, waxing and waning, until 1914, when the Ottoman Empire joined with Germany to face France, Britain, and Russia and the fate of Palestine was put on hold.

Four years later, with the Germans and their allies defeated and on their knees, the spoils of war were divided at Versailles. Part of Britain's prize was to be given, in the form of a Mandate, that area of the near and middle East, which included the country of Palestine. All in all, a mixed blessing. Access to the oil riches of the area was, decidedly important, but with that, they also inherited all the feuds, both the little nasty local ones between one tribe and another over who owns the well, but also the almost insolvable problem between Jew and Arab. Here they were then, when Cecil arrived in 1935.

ASSIGNMENT IN THE DESERT...

The days passed. Cecil was contented. Things were relatively quiet and he enjoyed being in the country and in the city. He traveled a good deal and visited Jerusalem and Jaffa. He met some of the families on both sides, who pretty well ran things, and he got on well with them. He learned more about the situation there and became fairly well-versed with all points of view. He was able to settle some tricky matters involving land lots and rights-of-way, and was becoming known and liked amongst the locals. He kept active playing tennis and squash and swimming in the sea on weekends at a lovely spot with a Saracen Castle called Athlit. He went to a variety of social events, met people, including a lot of pretty girls, many out from England, where they were in school, now on holiday with their parents, who worked in Palestine or were in the military or diplomatic corps.

One morning Cecil was sitting idly flicking his fly swat at some pesky bluebottles in his office and thought, 'I wish they would send me out on my own next trip.' Up to now his travels had always been with either Davies or some other more senior officer.

The phone rang.

"New orders for you Paynter. Come to my office would

you?" It was the chief. Could this be it?

"Come in." The raspy voice of Murdoch answered his knock. Cecil opened the door and went in.

"Ah, come in Paynter. I want you to meet this gentleman." A tall dark man in a light tan suit sat in the other chair. He got up and held out his hand as Cecil approached. Cecil took it and they made their greetings.

"How do you do?" said Cecil.

"Shalom," said the stranger.

"Paynter, this is Mr. Robert Nadel. He's in charge of immigration control under the temporary arrangements we have with the Jewish Agency at this time. I want you to get to know each other, as you will be working with each other to try to make things easier under the rather sticky circumstances we're in at present."

"Yes sir," said Cecil, standing stiffly to attention.

"Relax man. Sit down." He motioned to the only other chair in the room which was not stacked with books.

"Thank you sir." He sat down.

Murdoch spoke first.

"Mr. Nadel is going on a fact-finding trip and we think you should go with him. It will be good experience for you and you will be able to see things from their point of view. Your familiarity with some of the locals will come in useful too."

"When would we be going sir?" asked Cecil.

"Next week," interposed Nadel. "On Monday. I've set up meetings with some of Daud's people."

Cecil knew that these were especially troubling tribes

and that they were dead against any allowed Jewish immigration.

"That's starting with a really tough one." Cecil smiled wryly.

"Yes. That's why I chose them to be first," said Nadel.

Monday came with the usual blazing sun and cobalt sky. Although it was still early in the day at this time of the year, mid June, the heat seared.

Nadel and his entourage met Cecil at his hotel and they all sipped coffee in the little room for visitors on the ground floor. The good Signora bustled about. She had grown fond of Cecil and looked with some suspicion at his new companions.

Many of the transplanted Christian Europeans looked without favour on the possibility of a Jewish state in Palestine. Up to now all the different factions, Jew, Christian, and Arab had lived in harmony. They knew that this equation was delicate and could easily be disturbed by any imbalance, which was, they thought, sure to come.

Cecil and Nadel walked out to the car, which was already occupied by two tough-looking characters who turned out to be members of the Jewish unofficial military, the Haganah. They glared at Cecil when he said good morning and ignored his salutation.

"Where is everyone going to fit in?" asked Cecil, looking around at the others coming out with them.

"Oh, they are not coming," said Nadel diffidently. "Just the four of us. Are you armed?"

"Yes," said Cecil indicating his holstered revolver.

"Good. One never knows."

Cecil looked at him in astonishment.

"I hope you and your," he hesitated, "friends, are not. We cannot go into the Bedou camps bristling with guns. They would view that with great suspicion."

"Don't worry old boy," Nadel said in a stage English accent and with a mocking tone of voice, "we won't embarrass you, you and your Arab chums." The other two grinned.

"Alright boys let's go. We have to be at the camp in a couple of hours."

Cecil looked at him grimly and lit a cigarette. They drove in silence.

The road wound out of town into the dusty hills. 'When one gets out of the towns and cultivated areas this really is a desperately ugly country,' thought Cecil. 'Oh for England and its wet greenness.' Craggy, stunted trees and shrubs all layered with a coat of sand gave a universal brownness to the world surrounding them. The whole impression was one of depressing lifelessness.

They breasted a rise and began a descent that mirrored the climb they had just completed. The land some several hundreds of feet ahead and below them, looked drab and hopeless. The sky was a copper colour and glared down on them pitilessly. Some large black birds with ragged wings like vultures circled around overhead and to their right.

"How much further?" Cecil asked.

"Nearly there," said Nadel.

They drove for another hour, then reached a small

village, just a huddle of mud huts and some tents. This, it seemed, was the home of Daud.

The driver pulled up outside one of the bigger huts. A tall, bearded Arab strode out. He did not look happy, but saluted Cecil.

"*Salaam aleikum, ya,*" he said to Cecil. "You are welcome."

Cecil returned the greeting. This was the son of the Emir and an important man in his own right. Nadel and his men got out of the car and came up behind them. Abdullah, for that was the Bedou's name, looked at them with an expression of severity.

"These men however, are not welcome." At that point several other Arabs came out to join them. They all looked grim and handled the daggers in their sashes in a threatening manner.

"*Ya Salaam,*" said Cecil, in tone that indicated surprised alarm and acknowledged the greeting.

"There has been an incident at Ras Sahadi," a village Cecil knew was not far away.

"Some of these people have killed grape growers there. We cannot deal with the matters planned. You must go away now."

"Very well," said Cecil. "I am sorry for your troubles. We shall leave."

"What's the problem?" asked Nadel. Cecil told him.

"Apparently some of your people have killed some grape growers at a village near here. We are not having any discussions here today. In my opinion we should bugger off out of here before things get ugly."

The powerful engine in the Humber they were driving, propelled them out of the village in a cloud of rather undignified dust.

"Well, what now?" One of Nadel's henchmen turned in his seat and looked back at them.

"We return to Haifa and make new plans. How are we for petrol?"

"Oh, not too good. Not enough to get home."

"I didn't see any stations on the way did you George?"

"No," answered henchman number two. "So what do we do?"

"I have a suggestion," said Cecil.

"What is it?"

"I have friends in Hayil which is not far from here. How much petrol do we actually have?"

"About half a tank."

"Oh that's plenty. We can stay the night there and rest, and go on tomorrow."

"Okay."

They reached the little village half an hour later and were met, not with the usual hospitality of the country, but with a fusillade of gun fire. The driver clapped the brakes on and the car skidded into a drainage ditch and rolled onto its back. Cecil felt an enormous feeling of *deja vu* and a resounding bang on his head. He was hurled from the back seat onto the hard ground where he lay for a second or two, trying to gather his wits about him.

The gun fire had stopped, so he carefully peered about. Someone was lying further down the ditch. From the colour of the suit he guessed it was Nadel. 'Where were the other two?'

He looked back to where the car was and could just see a body hanging out of one of the windows. He struggled to get to his feet but his legs wouldn't support the effort. A pain through his right knee made him look down. It looked oddly crooked. At that moment, with a great whomp, the car blew up in an incandescent explosion of yellow and orange flame, and then an eruption of oily black and brown smoke, then bits of things fell about him as he tried to bury himself into the ground. Then all went black and he was falling into a whirling vortex of roaring sound and velvety night.

"Are you alright sir?" An anxious cockney voice spoke somewhere in another world.

"What?" Another voice seemed to answer. It sounded like his voice only older and as though far away. He felt a cool dampness on his face.

Someone was dabbing at his head with a cloth soaked in water. He lifted his hand but heard a voice say "There, there sir, just rest easy, you'll be alright."

He opened his eyes. A large red-faced soldier, wearing a scarlet and blue forage cap, was looking at him with a look of worried concern.

" 'Ee's come to sergeant."

"Right. Let's 'ave a look."

Another burly figure came into Cecil's limited view.

"Can you talk sir?"

"Yes. I'm alright. Just a bit of a headache. What happened?"

"Well sir, looks like you was ambushed by the bloody Arabs. We 'eard the shooting and came over to 'ave a look We found you lying 'ere with the other gentleman standing over you with two guns in 'is 'ands. 'Ee was blazing away real fierce, like a cowboy movie. It was the Arabs were the Redskins as it were. I reckon 'ee saved your life. Quite the 'ero."

'My God, that must have been Nadel.'

"Where is the gentleman."

"Oh 'ee was in bad shape sir. We sent 'im off to Haifa in one of the cars."

"Thank you sergeant. So who are you?"

"11th 'ussars, sir."

"Well done. The cavalry to the rescue again eh?"

"That's right sir. This way sir. 'Ere's the car." They helped him to the armoured car standing nearby. Cecil got in and sat down awkwardly. Pain coursed through his leg.

"I think I've broken my leg."

"Looks like it sir. We'll get you the 'orspital in no time. Just rest there. 'Orl right driver. Off we go. Nice and easy now. No bumps if you please."

As Cecil felt another pain in his leg he instinctively put his hand down to grasp the hurt and his hand brushed his revolver holster. It was unbuttoned and empty.

"I say sergeant what happened to the revolvers Mr. Nadel

was using?"

"Oh we got them sir." Oddly enough one of them was an officer's service Webley."

"Oh, I see," said Cecil. He smiled to himself.

Deja Vu...

After several weeks in hospital Cecil was well enough to report back to work. The chief had him in his office and advised him to take things easy for a while, partly for convalescent reasons and partly because any more efforts of them trying to bring the two sides together were to be on hold indefinitely. New plans were afoot in London, and talks were underway to decide what it was that HMG could do to improve a steadily worsening situation. It was the autumn of 1935.

Meanwhile, Cecil took things easy, spending much of his time exploring all the other amenities of the area. He went one Sunday afternoon to a rather staid tea party put on by one of the local characters who had taken him under her wing. She was an ex-show girl from London who had married into one of the great families in England and was now a widow, a Lady Dowager actually. She had a presence in the area and gave many good parties. This was one of her quieter ones, given for some of the young people on leave from home.

Cecil wasn't sure why he had been asked, and was wondering how soon he could politely leave, when a voice in his ear said "Would you like a cup of tea Sir?"

Cecil turned and almost fainted. It was Susan! Or at least a younger version, but there were the eyes, the shape of face, the complexion, the mouth and nose.

He stammered "Er, thanks. Thank you," and took the cup and saucer from her hands. She smiled and walked away. He lit a cigarette and tried to pull himself together. 'Who is she?' The resemblance was so striking he was convinced she must be some sort of relative He sought out Dolly, the Dowager. He found her looking trapped between a priest and two nuns.

"Excuse me Dolly. Can we talk."

"So sorry Father. My apologies, Sisters."

The priest with little finger cocked at the tea cup pursed his lips and looked disapproving. The Nuns glowered with little icy blue eyes, and all turned away.

"Thanks darling. You saved my life," laughed Dolly.

"Listen dear, who is that?" He motioned towards the girl who was crossing the room with a plate of sandwiches.

"Oh that's Maggie. She's the daughter of a rather sweet Canadian woman who's out here with her husband. His name is Nadel, a very big man in the Zionist movement here. They say he'll really be somebody if they ever take over."

"Well this is extraordinary." Cecil told her the story.

"My God. That's fantastic. I'll send for her right away." She went to the telephone in the hall and talked to someone.

Cecil was feeling numb.

"Okay." Dolly came back. "She's home. I didn't say anything except that I had a surprise for her."

An hour or so later the party was breaking up, all the families leaving. Cecil was sitting smoking nervously, wondering... , wishing he could have a drink, when he heard her voice. It was true. She was here. He jumped up as she came in followed by Dolly, grinning from ear to ear.

"My God, Cecil!"

"My darling. What are you doing here?"

They fell into each others arms. She was laughing and crying all at the same time. Then, as if this wasn't enough, in came Maggie looking startled and confused.

"Sweetheart," said Susan, "come and meet your father."

Pandemonium reigned. Everyone hugged, kissed, wept, including Dolly, who streamed tears and waltzed around the room with a startled Arab servant. All the staff came running out of the kitchen, the chef too, a very dignified Armenian with large mutton chop whiskers, who, not caring what the celebration was about began to whirl about like a Dervish.

When it all calmed down, Dolly yelled, "Achmed. Bring out the good champagne. Everybody will toast this great occasion. Glasses. Now, you three. Here's to love!"

They celebrated until late. Cecil and Susan stayed together at his hotel. They clung to each other until dawn.

Next morning, at his desk, the books and papers and files seemed less attractive now. Not surprisingly, Cecil found it impossible to concentrate on matters that yesterday seemed of paramount importance. All he could think of now were Susan and Maggie and how his life had suddenly taken a new direction. Though immeasurably happy with all that had happened, he felt uneasy about how his appearance in their lives would be disturbing. Susan was married to a man about to make his name in the political whirlpool of the area. She was obviously supportive of his views. Maggie was a normal, loving pre-teen in the middle of her school days. How would all this complicate her life?

Susan had made her feelings plain. She was ready to go to her husband and ask for a separation. She had no doubts at all about who she wanted to be with. Cecil knew things were not that simple though. Beside all these complications, Susan's husband was the man who had just saved Cecil's life.

Cecil wondered about all this. In any case, there would soon be a short separation, as Susan was going to Egypt to take Maggie to Port Said where she was to join the boat taking her back to England, school holidays being over. Susan would be gone for a week. While she was there, her husband would meet her and return to Haifa with her. It would give Cecil a chance to think things through.

The next few days before they left were spent close together, nights and days. They would meet Maggie early in the morning, and, as Cecil had scrounged a couple of days off, they went everywhere together. They drove to the top of Mount Carmel, which overlooked the city, and where the B'Hai faith was headquartered. They swam in the lovely glistening sea and had picnics. They went to cafes and night clubs. They danced and loved and laughed. They lived as if the world might end tomorrow.

However, the sad day arrived for them to leave each other. At the station, Maggie clung to Cecil and wept. Susan hugged them both. Cecil tried to make reassuring comments about their futures together, but felt as though he might break down completely and disastrously. He prayed for the train to leave before this happened.

The whistle blew. The doors began to slam up and down

the train. The engine gave its odd little hoot, and they kissed goodbye. Cecil watched as the train clanked out of the station, then turned to go.

Probably it was because his eyes were full of tears that he didn't see the Arab come from behind a barrow of luggage and point a pistol at him, firing two shots at point blank range. He felt the impact like a heavy blow against his chest and shoulder and fell to his knees, conscious only of a feeling of sad unreality and loud noises that might have been shouting.

Cecil woke with a feeling of surreal vacancy. He felt strangely disconnected and dreamy. Then he heard a sound like a girl, far away, giggling. Then, as he gradually came out of his drugged state, a cross voice saying "Stop that noise nurses. There's a young man near death in this room."

That comment made Cecil concentrate forcibly and brought him to his senses. 'Bugger that. I'm not ready to die yet.' He tried to call out, but only managed a weak croak. It was enough though, as the nursing sister came into his line of sight.

"How do you feel?"

More croaks from Cecil. Then he managed to say "Water please sister."

She held a glass to his parched lips. He drank gratefully.

"Not too much, you've got an internal wound. You are a very lucky young man."

"I got shot didn't I?"

"You did. Twice. One, a flesh wound in the shoulder. The other is a nasty one in the upper chest. Ah doctor." She looked up as a white-smocked man with a stethoscope around his neck walked in.

"How's our patient Sister?"

"Surprisingly well doctor. He's just woken up."

"How long have I been out?" asked Cecil.

"Two days my boy. We were getting a bit anxious. But I think with a few weeks rest you will be alright. You are young and in good health. The chest wound seems to be clearing up. There was a little infection, but that seems to be clearing up now too. Alright Sister, put him back to sleep. I'll be in first thing in the morning. We'll decide what to do then."

The next few days and nights passed in a blur that tasted of copper, and with dreams that made him wake, shouting and shaking. Then, one night, he woke to feel cool hands comforting and gentle.

"What, what is it?"

"It's alright my darling it's me. I will look after you now."

"Susan! My dear. Oh how wonderful. I thought I'd gone and you were an angel."

"Well you've not gone and I'm no angel. I'm staying with you forever. Just relax and go back to sleep."

'Oh what heaven.' He floated back into darkness.

HOME...

The great day came when he knew he was better. He felt awake, clearheaded, without pain, hungry, thirsty, and wanting to leap out of bed and take on the world. But where was Susan? He had to see her. The door opened and the nurse came in.

"Ah," she said. "I see you have decided to join us. How do you feel now?"

"Oh, terrific," said Cecil. "I want to get up. But where's Mrs. Nadel?"

"Well she had to go home for a rest. She will be back later. Alright how about a real bath instead of damp cloths and sponges in bed?"

"Sounds heavenly. Lead on sister."

Later that day Susan came to see him. She looked serious.

"What's the matter my dear?" Cecil asked.

"I've told Robert all about us and of my feelings."

"Oh? How did he take it, as if I don't know."

She looked at him.

"Oh my dear it was awful. I don't know what to do."

Cecil paused a long time. He had been thinking for a long time while in his hospital bed.

"Well I do. We must end this. Your life with him and Maggie is more important. He has serious work to do here and

242

you must support him. I'm a copper. God knows where I'll be sent to next. They frown on wives anyway. The chances are that after this they will send me back to England to recover. No my darling, we have to face facts." He held her hand and looked into her eyes.

She said "I know you are right, but it's so unfair."

As if to save any further distress the doctor walked in and said "Good news. They are sending you back to Blighty. I don't know why really. I told them you would be quite alright here, in time, but they want to make some sort of hero of you. There's talk of a medal of some kind. So anyway, you leave tomorrow."

"But what about my work?"

"Oh they will no doubt send you back here after they have finished with you."

"Oh. That's alright then."

"Right. Well. I'll leave you to it then. Get your stuff together. Say your goodbyes." He looked kindly at Susan. "Transport will be laid on to the airfield. They are even flying you home. You must really be someone."

Of course an enormous party was laid on that night, so it was a delicate Cecil that they helped onto the Imperial Airways Hercules next morning. He had said his farewells to a tearful Susan after the party, when they had stayed together at his hotel. They had both stayed awake most of the night, and finally had cried themselves to sleep.

Now, looking out of his small window, Cecil waved to the little group of friends who had come to see him off. They were standing by the buildings. All the little arms waved. He saw Driscoll, the Irishman, waving his cap.

Ahead and below, he saw the officer in charge of ground movement make a hand signal to the pilot who was powering up. Then the ground officer come to attention and saluted, as was the custom in those days. The brakes were released. They moved forward, slowly at first, then faster and faster, until Cecil felt the tail come up. Then the big bird left earth and soared into space, the blue green transparent sea flashing by below. Cecil sighed and went to sleep.

While Cecil slept, the great aircraft continued its flight that had begun at Bombay, stopped for fuel at Habaniya in Iraq, then Palestine, now to Rome, then to Paris, and the last leg to complete the journey, to Lympne in Kent. When he finally woke somewhere over the French Alps, Cecil realised that he was not as fit as he had thought. He felt, in fact, bloody awful. He considered a drink but the thought nauseated him. 'God! I must really be sick,' he thought. He instead, adjusted the pillow the steward had given him, and went back to blessed oblivion.

The rest of the trip passed in a sort of blur of surreal pictures. He was vaguely aware of being woken to tighten belts for a landing that might have been Rome. He wasn't sure. He was aware only that it was dark and flashing lights played on his face. Then he slept again. Then there was more commotion. Voices. Someone holding his hand. No, holding his wrist. A cool smooth object was slipped into his mouth and under his tongue. A deep voice said something garbled. His head was raised and held. Someone told him to drink. A pleasant tasting liquid was poured down his throat, which felt sore and hot. Then, unconsciousness.

An ambulance waited on the tarmac when the plane landed and Cecil was carried off the plane on a stretcher. It was raining. He felt the blessed, cool, damp, greenness on his face. He had come home.

Inside the ambulance he was strapped in, the attendants checking belts and buckles.

"Nice and comfy sir?"

Cecil groaned.

"That's right sir. Soon have you tucked in, in 'horspital. S'pect they'll give you a saucy nurse and all. Blimey."

Cecil felt faintly sick. A big black hole swallowed him into a vortex of hallucination. He dreamt again. Images sped by... . He dreamt of people in uniforms... .

Everyone wore a uniform in those days. Postmen wore a funny shako on their heads. It had twin peaks front and back. The London Fire Brigade wore helmets of brass that looked like the French Cuiraisseurs at Waterloo. When off duty they wore caps like sailors, with no peak at all. They also were dressed in tunics with a double row of brass buttons down the front.

All the police forces wore different uniforms. The London area had two forces, one, the well-known Metropolitan Police, and the other, the City Of London Force wore a higher helmet and a stand-up collar.

The park keepers who patrolled the green spaces of

London wore a brown, tweedy, rather bucolic outfit with a brown bowler hat and leggings. They were rather unkind to little boys trying to climb trees and run on the grass.

The milk companies were all dressed differently: the United Dairies in orange and white, the Express Dairies in blue and white. But all the cheerful milk men wore striped aprons and whistled a lot, with their amiable horses clip-clopping along beside.

There seemed to be a lot of nurses and nuns about in extraordinary costumes. The nurses were in military orders, the QAINS (Queen Alexandra's Imperial Nursing Services), the VADs (Voluntary Aid Detachment), the FANYs (Field Ambulance Nursing Yeomanry) in greys, khakis, blues, and scarlet. Both the nurses and the nun's headgear ranged from a simple little cone perched prettily atop the head, to complicated wimpole-like winged constructions of waving white, which shadowed their faces into mystery. Those in holy orders were often young novitiates twittering like birds and scurrying along in little groups with shiny black shoes.

The saddest uniforms were the shabby, shiny, threadbare suits worn by the halt and the lame, the leftovers from the battlefields of France and Flanders. They sat and knelt outside the tube stations with their chalked pictures on the pavement and the inevitable up-turned cap with a scattering of pennies in it, some with a card-sign hanging around their necks attesting to the fact that they had been gassed at Ypes or wounded at Pilkem Ridge.

At a sudden jerk he awoke, almost cast onto the floor.

His head was aching.

"God. Can't you drive a little slower?" he croaked.

"Sorry sir. Orders are we 'ave to get you to 'orspital in London fast."

"Where the hell are we?" asked Cecil.

"Elephant and Castle sir. We're going to Lambeth. Not far now."

"Thank God," sighed Cecil, and he passed out again.

Thirty minutes later the vehicle drew up at the hospital emergency doorway and the process of unloading began. Cecil was wheeled up interminable yellow-lit corridors. Many doors swung open and shut. A room full of the usual hospital impedimenta and with a tiny bed was entered. Cecil was laid gently on it. He opened his eyes gingerly, it was dark. A figure bent over him with a faint fragrance of lavender.

A soft voice said "My darling. Don't worry. I'm going to look after you now." It was Rowena...

ACKNOWLEDGMENTS

Thank you to all these talented people who helped put the Devil in his place...

...to my wonderful, generous publisher Mark Salmonowicz, whose engineering skills were put to good use in getting us all together on the same page with such precision and patience.

...to my dear friend John Lederman who, again, patiently and cleverly edited my scrawl and arranged words and music to come up with, in my opinion, such an attractive production.

...to Mr. Christopher Plummer who took time out to help and encourage me and to allow his name to be used in the reviews.

...to Ms. Tyler Addison-Colins who read the rough manuscript and made comments of inestimable worth and, as well, added her comments to the reviews.

...to Ms. Maryann Cox who allowed us to grace our cover with her beauty.

...to Bob Newland and John Woodward at Fanfare Books for being so helpful in matters pertaining to sales and promotion and being such peerless advisers on all matters literary.

...to my good friends Jim and Joan Schiele who read the manuscript while driving route 66 to St. Louis, one driving the other reading aloud. Thanks Schieles for your annotations, comments, and suggestions.

BIOGRAPHY

Teddy Payne, a well-known bon vivant and raconteur now living in Stratford, Ontario, was born and raised in eastern England, and has worked, traveled and lived around the world. He now spends his time writing and creating original watercolors, which are on display in his downtown Stratford gallery. He is knowledgeable about military history and his expertise is often sought on this and other subjects.

Further reading from Edward Payne

The *Apricot Blooms In The Desert*
A Literary Memoir, Part One

The *Streets Of Odeon*
A Literary Memoir, Part Two

Teddy Payne's *Restaurants Of Stratford*
A Guide Book With Recipes

Available from:

Fanfare Books
92 Ontario Street
Stratford, Ontario, Canada, N5A 3H2
519.273.1010
fanfare@cyg.net